WHEN A TIGON WEDS

A LION'S PRIDE #9

EVE LANGLAIS

A
LION'S
PRIDE
THE SERIES

CHAPTER ONE

T was' a clear and lovely night. Unlike Dean's mood, which churned with memory.

On a night much like this one, he'd gotten his lovely, striped tail with its fantastic tuft, royally yanked. Not literally. He'd have shredded anyone who even dared to pull his most excellent tigon tail. Yank... figuratively. He'd been fooled by someone he thought he could trust. Blame a lack of blood to his brain. He was always hard around her. Perpetually stupid.

In his defense, Natasha had a way of moving. A certain smile. A tilt of her head. The way she cocked her hip... All of it designed to enflame. To render him witless.

But he was wise to her games now. Knew her strengths and weaknesses. He couldn't wait until the rematch.

He poured himself a glass of whiskey—the expensive kind that he could sip all night long, given how smooth it tasted. He paced himself. It wouldn't do to get drunk or to pass out too soon. Tonight was the night.

Natasha was coming. He could feel it in the marrow of his bones. He just needed to be patient. Wait for her to make a move. Given what he knew about her, surely it wouldn't be long now.

He'd been following her movements ever since she'd played him for a fool. It proved easier than expected, given she was quite active on social media. Although, that didn't mean much given staged photos could be scheduled to release ahead of time to give the appearance of an active life.

Dean knew how easy it was to fake. For example, according to one very popular site that just allowed pictures with hashtags, Dean was currently in a bar, having a few drinks.

Would she fall for it? Would she think him away from home?

Doubtful. Just like he didn't believe the last image he'd seen of her on a beach soaking up the sun's rays. She didn't vacation in some tropical place. She was nearby. Getting closer.

Or was that just wishful thinking?

Dean grabbed his phone and pulled up her profile, still displaying that same beach pic. She wore a sleek one-piece bathing suit with a single shoulder strap. Over it, she'd loosely tied a sarong. She'd barely changed since he'd last seen her. Her hair was the same style, her skin just as fresh. She looked so youthful, and yet, she was only five years younger than he.

Despite what he knew of her, she remained beautiful. While he liked to think her betrayal would render him immune to her charms, one look, and he immediately became stupid.

Case in point, look at him, having a few drinks, expecting Natasha to stop by. He knew she'd come to find him eventually. But waiting took patience. Good thing he'd practiced for hours at a time. Hours he'd spent hunkered in the tall grass, a hiding tigon ready to pounce. He'd learned to never scare his aunts like that, given the one time he'd made Aunt Marni pee herself, and she chased him down and shaved his mane. One did not irritate the aunts. Or the cousins either for that matter. They would plot the most heinous revenge.

Another glass of whiskey, and still no Natasha.

More than three days had passed since he'd seen the announcement online. *Proud to announce the upcoming nuptials of...* In black and white text with a colored image of the smiling couple as proof.

Natasha was getting married.

Maybe.

Dean had a thing or two to say about it, which was why, after pounding back a large bottle of whiskey, he'd sent her a note. A reminder of their unfinished business.

The next day, he'd received a registered letter,

addressed to him from a lawyer, demanding his signature. An impersonal way of concluding matters.

Nope. Dean burned the letter and didn't bother sending a reply. The tigon waited some more. He had his home cleaned top to bottom. Got a haircut. A new suit.

Two more demands arrived from the lawyers. He set those documents on fire too, in the yard with a can of lighter fluid and a match. He used more fuel than necessary, on purpose. As it flared bright, he lit his cigar from the dancing flames, and when it puffed nicely, he used it to salute the hovering drone that had been watching his property all day. He winked before pulling out a gun and shooting it out of the sky.

If Natasha wanted to see him, she could come in person. He waited some more. Painted his bedroom. Pumped some weights. Stripped the wallpaper with his claws and then replastered the whole thing.

At nine thirty-two, his watch buzzed. A glance was all it took for him to grin. "Showtime."

The empty glass needed a top-up. Once he'd filled the tumbler halfway, Dean chose to sit in the gray club chair in the center of his living room, which implied a livelier place than reality. White walls to his left and right with a lofty, white ceiling. To his back, the kitchen, with its massive island and wood cupboards. In front, an enormous sliding glass window that opened to a patio.

The interlocked stone was faintly visible due to

the illuminated infinity pool. Built on a cliff, he enjoyed floating on the surface, feeling as if he were part of the sky—he could only hope the rock face would never shear away, although the danger did add to the enjoyment of his backyard oasis.

He'd chosen to wait inside in comfort, reclining in his chair, placing his glass on the metal column beside it, shaped to appear as a log, that acted as a table. If he pressed a button on the armrest to his left, a screen would drop from the ceiling, allowing him to watch television. He left the tele off, though he did momentarily debate throwing on some tunes. But what would he play? Something soft and sensual, or hard and action-packed?

He took another sip of whiskey, enjoying the heat of it as it went down, and waited.

Smash.

The sliding glass door shattered as something hit it hard. Glass sprayed over the hardwood and rolled across the buffalo hide carpet—a real one he should add. Dean had taken it off a sadistic hunter—right after Dean made him repent every animal he'd tortured.

Despite the hole in his window, Dean took another gulp of whiskey. Liquid courage that hopefully might slow down the flow of blood from his brain elsewhere.

Stay smart. He feigned nonchalance he didn't feel. Hummed with adrenaline.

It was time.

A figure swung into the room, concealed head to

toe in dark garments including a face mask and a swaddling hood. The rope snapped loose as they landed on their feet. Interesting tactic, using his roof. A good thing he'd installed sensors there last year.

The slight figure didn't hold any weapon, and their features were masked but he didn't need to see to know. He tingled. His beast shivered and almost uttered a rumbling noise.

"Hello, Natasha. Long time, no see."

She swung her hips as she stalked towards him. "Don't you mean since our wedding night?"

Less wedding, more hoax. Natasha hadn't married him because he was the best thing since peanut butter and chocolate got together. She used him.

He tamped down his anger and remained cool as he said, "What's it been, five months? Six?" He could have quoted the exact time down to the minute had he wished. He kept his tally to himself. He'd never give her that kind of power. And, so far, so good. He still had his wits about him.

Her hands tucked behind her back. "Too long and overdue. I'm here to ask for a divorce."

Despite expecting this, he couldn't help a growl. Given the lies she'd told him, he should be happy that she wanted to end the false marriage. Yet, a part of him had known then, and knew even more strongly now.

She is mine.

More than ever, he was convinced of it, and yet she didn't appear to have the same struggle as he did. He'd been fighting the urge to hunt her down ever since that night. He wouldn't be the one to go begging. The one to admit weakness.

Which was why he waited. Why he bided his time. He'd wagered that one day she'd return if only to ask him for a divorce.

He had pictured this moment in so many different ways, some of them ending in naked passion. But in every instance when she asked him to sever their marriage, his answer remained the same. *No.*

Never.

He wouldn't agree even if she seduced him right this second and made him purr.

He arched a brow. "Is this where I say I believe the vow was until death do us part?"

"If you insist." The hand behind her back emerged, lifting a gun that she held level with his face.

"I take it you got my note." The one that was basic and said, *Here's a copy of our marriage certificate.* Signed, *Your husband.*

"We are not married."

"I see you're surprised. So was I when I realized you weren't who I thought."

"That wedding was a sham," she growled.

"Perhaps to you. And yet, vows were exchanged."

"I left before it was done."

"Apparently not soon enough, given I received a certificate in the mail two weeks later."

"Why didn't you tell me when you got the notice?"

Natasha shoved up the face covering, revealing her full-lipped glory. Her eyes a stormy sea.

His resolve began to slip. Still so damned gorgeous. He had to remain strong. He took another sip of liquid courage before saying, "I would have told you, but you disappeared and then didn't keep in touch."

"Because I was done with you," she exclaimed, waving the gun with clear exasperation.

"Maybe you were, but I still have unresolved issues with you, *wife*." He said it quite deliberately and enjoyed the spot of angry color that appeared in each of her cheeks. She was a liar and a fake, but he remained steadfast in his certainty that she belonged with him.

"Is this a male ego thing? Because I don't do those. I used you. Get over it. Don't get pissy with me because you didn't do your homework."

The sassy rebuke kept his blood where it belonged. "I would have eventually gotten around to doing a background check." Said in a grumble. Way to remind him of just how monumentally deficient he'd been. He'd not taken any kind of precaution. Hadn't once even thought of checking Natasha out more deeply. She'd fooled him so well. He admired her skill.

"If it makes you feel better, I never dug too deep with you either. I fell for your lazy playboy act."

That brought a smile to his lips. It turned out they had more in common than either of them realized.

"Who says it's an act?"

"Because I've been looking into you, as well. You're an interesting fellow, and your name isn't actually Dean." The gun she'd relaxed steadied in line with his heart.

It was a nickname given to him because some of his female family members decided that he reminded them of the television heartthrob on that show about the paranormal. He preferred it over his real name Neville Horatio Fitzpatrick.

"Would you really shoot me, Natasha?" he asked, not the least bit worried despite the steel in her expression. Surely, she felt the connection pulsing between them. The electricity. Or was that just pure hate? She certainly didn't seem to be softening.

"Either you agree to a divorce, or I'm going to suddenly become a grieving widow, Neville." She did on purpose to use the name he hated.

"You are more violent than I recall. What happened to the soft-spoken university student I met?" She'd been wide-eyed and shy in the bar where he'd first seen her. Sipping on her virgin piña colada, her shirt buttoned to her neck, her skirt covering her knees. Her hair hanging loose with just a barrette holding it out of her face. She'd seen him looking and smiled, ducked her head. He'd completely fallen for her innocent act.

"You saw what you wanted to see. Just like every other man." Said with disdain, and he couldn't blame her. She was right. He'd only ever seen the luscious woman who made him feel like a big, bad tigon. She smelled just right, and even though she'd never shown him her beast side, he could sense the feline inside her, was attracted to it. Wanted to rub himself against her and smear her with his scent. Cordon off an area around her with some urine to mark her as his. Roar to everyone looking that she belonged to him.

She'd really fooled him.

"I'm surprised guns are your weapon of choice." Because he would have said her most dangerous weapon was her gentle touch. She had a way of rousing his passion and blinding him to the truth. And damn did it feel good.

"Guns. Knives. Pressure points. Poison." Her bow lips curved. "I had an interesting childhood." As the daughter of a renowned Russian mobster, of course, she had. Not that he'd known of her background when he met her. As far as he knew, he'd met Natasha Smirnoff, foreign student from Russia, orphaned and currently in America on a scholarship. A lone tigress with permission to be in the territory to study.

More lies. The Pride knew nothing about a Ms. Smirnoff. So many balls dropped, and rules broken.

As she listed off her mercenary capabilities, he lifted his glass in salute. "To the hidden depths of Natasha Tigranov. Anything else you'd like to add to the list?"

"I like to compete in archery and axe throwing competitions."

"But the question is, can you cook?" He already knew the reply.

"No."

"Then how on earth do you feed yourself?"

She scowled. "I have a chef."

"A chef?" He snorted. "Do you even know how to boil water?"

"Of course, I do. Scalding is one of the techniques I learned in my lessons on torture. Would you like me to show you?"

"Only if you're planning to make some fresh egg noodles. I do love my pasta." He patted his tummy.

"As if I'd cook for you."

"I'd say that's the wrong attitude to take, wife. Isn't pleasing your husband your job?" He deliberately threw out the most sexist thing he could think of. He was sure she'd shoot him. Her hand did shake a little, but she had great control.

"I am not your wife."

"I have proof claiming otherwise."

"I see I was correct in filing for divorce stating irreconcilable differences. A divorce I shouldn't even need, given that the wedding probably wasn't even legal."

"If it wasn't legal, then why couldn't your lawyer quash it?" He took another sip of his drink.

"He tried." Her lips flattened. "You ignored the letters we sent."

"You don't say." His glass was empty. To refill it

would require walking closer to her. It might be enough to tilt her over the edge. "Are you pouting because you didn't get your way?"

"I'm feeling murderous because you're being deliberately aggravating," she yelled. "I can't be married to you."

"Maybe you should have thought of that before you used me to get to my best friend!" He finally lost a bit of his temper. It wasn't enough that she'd fooled him and jilted him at the altar. She'd never been interested in him at all.

The smirk on her lips deepened. "Ah, are you still miffed over that teeny, tiny misunderstanding?"

He almost made a sound. "Tiny? You held a knife to Lawrence's throat." Which was surprising for a few reasons, the first being that she'd had a blade strapped to her leg in the first place.

"He lived." She didn't point out that it had come close.

"You used me!"

"We used each other. Quite often as I recall. In bed. Out of it." Each soft syllable she uttered acted as a reminder of those naked moments.

"Was it that often?"

"As if you've forgotten."

She was right, he remembered each moment. Vividly. But he wouldn't admit it. "The sex was decent, I guess."

"Decent?" She sputtered.

"You have to admit, it's been a while. And I have been seeing other women. Perhaps I need a refresher. Care to drop your pants so I can have a taste?"

Her nostrils flared, and her eyes narrowed. Remembrance and jealousy fought for supremacy on her features. Of course, she couldn't forget the pleasure he'd given her. She might have faked many things, but those clenching orgasms weren't one of them.

The petty feline part of him liked that he'd roused her anger by mentioning others. Not that there actually had been anyone since he'd met her. He'd tried to go on dates, not one ever made it to his bed. Their scent was wrong. Their smile not conniving enough.

"I'm not some slut to please your libido."

"You're my wife." He purred. "Isn't it your duty to service my husbandly needs?"

For a moment, he thought he might have tipped her over the edge. Her eyes flashed with anger. Only for a second, then a smug calm descended over her.

"I still can't believe you fell for the innocent schoolgirl routine." She batted her lashes as she taunted. "I've never felt this way before. Alas, it is not meant to be."

A reminder of how she'd pushed him to move quickly, declared herself head over heels with him, claiming with her student visa expiring, she'd have to leave him and go home.

He'd instantly proposed. She'd said yes. They flew to Vegas, and he'd only told his very close friend,

Lawrence, a liger who was in hiding but came out to be his best man.

Dean had led the enemy right to the door. It was pure luck that no one died on his wedding day. And not for a lack of trying. He still remembered the fragile feel of her throat in his hand.

CHAPTER TWO

That fateful night...

"I can't believe you came." Dean hugged his best friend, the only person he'd told about his upcoming nuptials.

"As if I'd miss you getting hitched!" Lawrence had dressed in a tux for the occasion, and if you ignored the bags under his eyes, he appeared in fine shape. He'd lost weight, though. Hiding from the mob would ruin the appetite.

"Wait until you meet Natasha. She's amazing," Dean had enthused. From the first time he'd laid eyes on her, he'd been captivated. He'd never imagined himself settling down, and certainly not with someone as sweet and innocent as she. But somehow, he knew he'd make it work.

Lawrence clapped him on the back. "I can't wait to get to know her."

And at the time, Dean couldn't wait to make Natasha his wife.

She'd dressed in white, the skirt long and flowing, the bodice tight, revealing the curves of her breasts. She'd kept her gaze downcast, and her steps mincing as she came down the aisle, bathed in disco light. In retrospect, he recognized her slight frown as she eyed the priest at Dean's back. A replacement given the original officiant had met with a mishap. Mainly, Dean not liking his face. He'd asked for a genuine-looking Elvis, not the gorilla in sequins they'd sent.

A good thing a new officiator could be rented and swapped in quickly. The ceremony unfolded with Natasha barely looking at him. When he grabbed the rings, she'd made her move.

She tore free her veil and tossed it just as he turned. The frothy fabric of it tangled around his head. By the time he ripped away the tulle enough to see, Natasha had already gone airborne, a knife in her left hand, the surprise and momentum of the move taking Lawrence to the floor. There, his friend pinned under her body, she'd placed the tip of her dagger on his throat.

It took Dean a few shocked blinks before he managed to say, "Natasha, what are you doing?"

She never once looked back at him as she growled. "The randy liger knows why I'm here."

"Wait, you know Lawrence?" He frowned. That

made no sense given his friend hadn't given any indication of recognition upon seeing her.

"Someone was a bad boy," she murmured. "But rather than man up, he hid."

The statement only worsened Dean's confusion. "Lawrence, I thought you said the mob was after you." At the time, Dean had hammered him with questions, wanting to know how he'd angered the mob. Was it guns? Drugs? But Lawrence had refused to reply.

His friend barely swallowed as he said, "The mob *is* after me."

He glanced at Natasha, a woman who no longer looked innocent at all despite the remnants of her white dress. "You work for the bad guys?"

"*Bad* depends on what side you belong to. And I will add, this isn't work. This is about family."

"I didn't mean to upset Sasha," Lawrence declared.

"You made my cousin cry!" Natasha pressed the knife hard enough to break the skin.

A serious situation, and yet Dean laughed. "You're threatening to slit his throat because he and your cousin broke up?"

"He played her."

"I never promised her anything," Lawrence insisted.

"Doesn't make it right. I promised Sasha I'd fix things."

"Would you like ominous music with that threat?"

Dean reeled from the knowledge that he'd been played.

"That would actually be rather nice. Do you have a playlist?" Her lips curved into a sadistic smile and damn her for rousing his lust with it.

Wrong time. Wrong place. Apparently, wrong person. "How about instead of killing Lawrence, you find your cousin another boyfriend?"

"But that's not as much fun." Natasha pouted, and it might have seemed guileless if not for the steely glint in her gaze.

Who was this woman? Because she obviously wasn't just sweet Natasha, struggling student with no living family and the sweetest mouth.

This woman was hotter, and threatening his best friend, who obviously only held off for one reason.

Dean glanced at Lawrence and gave him a slight nod. *Go ahead.*

She must have had some gut sense, or her reflexes were just that good. When Lawrence shoved his knees between their bodies, she went cartwheeling away and landed in a crouch with her knife out and a smirk on her lips.

"I see someone has taken some self-defense lessons," she taunted as Lawrence rose to his feet.

She never looked at Dean. Not once. Didn't notice the biggest threat in that chapel. She kept her gaze on Lawrence, never noticing that Dean had begun circling behind her.

"Surely, we can talk about this," his friend said.

"I'd rather just stop you from breaking the hearts of young susceptible girls." She tossed the knife, and it only narrowly missed his friend.

But she didn't seem to mind as she pulled another blade from her bodice. Exactly how many did she have hidden on her person?

"I'm sure Sasha will get over me."

"Maybe, but I made her a promise. She said, *Tashy, the big, bad kitty made me sad.'* How could I say no?"

Dean almost laughed.

As for Lawrence, he'd yet to pull the gun he surely had concealed. Mostly because they were both conscious of the Elvis priest watching them. The very human priest. It was the reason he'd not striped out.

But Natasha didn't seem to care that they had an audience. "Are you going to make me chase you in a skirt, or take your punishment like a man?"

"Funny you should mention punishment." Dean growled as he lunged, meaning to wrap his fiancée in a hug. Only she danced out of reach.

"Now, now. No reason for you to get involved." She shook the blade of her knife at him.

"I'd say I got involved the moment we both showed up to say our I dos."

"I do believe I fooled you," she taunted.

In that respect, she was right. Usually, Dean proved more cautious. But one sniff of his mate, and he'd lost all ability to see reason. Even now, he wanted to put his mouth on her neck, not tear it out. He yearned to lavish it with kisses before making his way past the bodice of that gown.

"Speaking of being fooled. I might not have been entirely honest either."

"Meaning what?" she asked, finally keeping her gaze on Dean.

Lawrence took that opportunity to rush her from behind. Only she twirled, dropped to a knee, and threw her knife. It hit him in the upper shoulder, and he roared. His features began bristling, his body bulging, about to shift.

Elvis was chanting something about blue suede shoes and no place like home.

Dean shook his head. Not here. Not now. Lawrence hissed as he pulled the dagger free.

The single ring of a phone, chiming *Ave Maria*, had Natasha sighing. "I swear, her timing is shit." She answered with one hand while pulling forth yet another knife with her other. "What is it, Sasha? I'm kind of busy cleaning up your mess." She listened, her gaze bobbing between Dean and Lawrence.

Dean always prided himself on his great hearing, but even he couldn't decipher what was said. He only saw Natasha nod before she put the phone away and tucked the knife into her bodice.

"It's your lucky day! Sasha has found a new boyfriend and says while you are scum of the Earth, she looks forward to the day she sees you again because you are sure to be overcome with jealousy. You will suddenly realize how epic she is, and while she will initially deny you, in the end, you will have wild, sweaty sex."

Lawrence understandably blinked. "What?"

"She's saying you're not dying anymore, dumbass," Dean snapped. He'd gone past the point of shock into anger.

"Yay?" Lawrence stated, a hand clapped to his bleeding wound.

"You should go buy yourself a lottery ticket because this is your lucky day. It's not often one of my targets walks free," she announced.

The statement prompted Dean to ask, "Who are you, really?"

As if to make a mockery of the moment, Elvis chose to say, "Congratulations, she appears to be your wife."

"Shut up!" They both turned to the guy, who suddenly hugged his bedazzled bible to his chest.

It was Lawrence who realized it first. "Holy catnip balls. She's a Tigranov. I don't know how I didn't see it before."

"Tigranov? As in related to the Russian tiger family?" Dean had known she was a striped feline, but given that he'd believed her lie of being an orphan, he'd never dug into her roots any deeper.

"Not just any Tigranov, if it makes you feel better,"

she'd taunted. "The daughter of Sergeii Tigranov himself."

"You're the tsarina?" Lawrence huffed.

"In the flesh." She swept a mocking bow, and then Natasha laughed, not sounding at all like the shy girl he'd known. There was a husky element to the sound. A taunting quality with a hint of evil.

"Unbelievable. You lied to me the entire time."

"Don't whine just because you were fooled." She stood in her white wedding dress, still looking beautiful—actually *more* gorgeous with an aura of menace. She showed not an inch of fear despite antagonizing two capable men. It wasn't just caution about her skills that held Dean back, but who she was.

A princess. A mob princess.

A lie he let walk out of that church.

A woman that turned out to be his wife.

And despite his better judgement, his mate.

CHAPTER THREE

Why wasn't the jerk saying or doing anything? He sat in the chair staring at Natasha, meaning she had time to notice that he'd not changed one bit in the months since their fake marriage. Still handsome, his jaw as square as she recalled. His body thick and toned, also relaxed. The man appeared the height of insouciance as he sat there sipping his whiskey. Meanwhile, her heart thumped, and she found herself breathless without having actually exerted herself. He'd always had this effect on her. The jerk.

"Dear wife." He said it on purpose. "We shouldn't be bickering, not when you do me such honor by visiting. Although might I recommend in the future that you use the front door? After all, *mi casa es su casa.*"

To think he was her husband. In name only. All

their consummation had occurred before the wedding. She ground her teeth. "Don't call me that."

"What? Wife?" He smiled. All kinds of white pearlies, capable of soft, pleasurable nips, and tearing out of throats. She'd seen the pictures. She'd read his file—after the fact, and a little too late.

Her accidental husband was more than just a lazy tigon with too much money at his fingertips. He worked for the Pride Group. Hunted for them, actually. Was very good by all reports, and yet, he'd never seen her coming. It was a source of personal pride that she'd so thoroughly fooled him.

But now that he'd tricked her, she wasn't feeling so benevolent.

"You know that marriage was a mistake. It was never supposed to be real." When Lawrence went into hiding, the only lead she'd had was a guy known as Dean, the man's best friend. She'd planned a fake wedding in order to get Lawrence to reappear in a vulnerable spot where she could make her point. Because she needed to make a point. Mess with one Tigranov, mess with them all. They were the bogeymen that shifters feared. The ones that kept their secrets safe and meted out justice if they were slighted in the least. She was one of their enforcers.

"Well, if you don't like *wife*, then I guess I'll just go back to my old nickname for you. *Baby*." He made a mockery of the sound.

Once upon a time, she'd enjoyed hearing him say

it. Now, it grated. "You're really pushing it, given I'm the one holding a gun."

"Which is surprising. I would have thought you'd have tried to gut me old school, like you tried to do to Lawrence. Remember, the best man at our wedding? The guy you tried to kill."

"But didn't." She'd never intended to actually kill him, that would have caused complications. But put the fear of the Tigranov family in him? Most definitely. A bit of maiming usually went a long way.

"You used me."

"Are you going to caterwaul about that again?" She rolled her eyes.

"Hell, yes, I'm going to complain. You convinced me to marry you to draw Lawrence out of hiding."

"You can say it. It was a brilliant plan until someone decided to replace my fake priest with a real one," she said with a glare.

"Some of us were going for the authentic Elvis wedding experience. The pictures came out great, by the way."

She gritted her teeth, not because she disagreed. He'd sent a photo with his note, and she did look pretty damned good. "I want those images destroyed, followed by your agreement to an annulment."

A smile tugged at his lips, and it heated parts of her that it shouldn't. "Why would I do that? I, for one, want to remember that most special of days."

"Why?"

"Unlike you, I meant it when I promised until death do us part."

"I should shoot you, right here, right now and save myself the annoyance of a divorce." Her anger snapped out the words.

"Living up to your family name?"

"There's a reason why I'm Papa's favorite." Her brother was a no-good wastrel, and her sister an insipid twit.

"Ah, yes, your papa. Does he know about our marriage?"

"No, and you better hope he never finds out. If you think I'm protective of my cousin, you should see how he is about me."

"I hardly see how marriage is a bad thing."

"You never asked his permission."

That got him to raise a brow. "Would he have agreed if I had?"

She eyed him. Then smiled slowly. "You'd never have made it out of his office alive. Papa isn't one for marrying outside our kind. Something about ensuring a strong family line."

"Funny because I'd always heard that bringing in fresh blood was the way to avoid three eyes and two tails."

The insult had her exclaiming, "We are not inbred."

"If you say so. I assume this means your father isn't

also your uncle and your brother and that your mother isn't your sister or aunt."

"That's gross."

"That's where my mind goes when you start talking about family dynasty and that shit."

"Well, you're wrong. There is quite a lot of thought put into the arranged consolidation of family lines."

He winced. "Way to make that sound completely unpleasant. I assume this is why you're engaged to *that boy*?" His lip curled in disdain.

On the one hand, she understood the derision. On the surface, her fiancé gave the appearance of a sop. Apparently, her fake husband hadn't realized he wasn't the only one with a social persona. "It's a good match." Approved by her father, that came with many perks for her.

"Does golden boy know you're a killer?"

Simon was from a very tawny branch of Siberian tigers, more blond than orange. Whereas the Tigranovs tended to range in hues, even striping in some cases brown and black. "Simon knows everything about me," she purred. "Every inch, sigh, and moan." She presented the lie and was rewarded by the spill of an angry growl as he reacted.

"Admitting to adultery, *baby*?" He visibly bristled. She'd finally struck a nerve. A jealous one.

She arched a brow. "Is it really adultery if we're both doing it?" Another fib. She'd not been with anyone since her time with Dean. Hadn't wanted to, which entailed her fabricating a story with Simon as to why they had to abstain. She'd told him he'd have to wait until their wedding night. Not that he'd ever pushed her. But how long would her fiancé remain content with a few chaste kisses?

Could she truly marry Simon and take him into her bed? Seeing Dean again, she feared the answer.

"Have you been keeping tabs on me?" he asked. "I'm flattered."

"Don't be. I research all my possible targets." When she couldn't forget him, she'd done some digging. Then, fascinated by what she found, she'd kept sporadic watch. Hating herself each time she went looking, and yet unable to stop herself from seeing what he was up to.

His public persona showed a devil-may-care bachelor—the façade that had fooled her before. It seemed at odds with the serious hunter for hire, who left no paper trail behind. But she'd seen reports of his work. Now knew what he was capable of.

A man like that wouldn't like being double-crossed, yet he'd left her alone this entire time. Waited for her because he knew she'd be back one day.

"Is your refusal to accept the annulment some kind of revenge? Are you really that petty?" She jabbed at him, poking at his pride.

"Revenge? On the contrary, our being married has been a blessing. No more hopeful mamas trying to snare me for their daughters. Just lovely ladies offering to console me because of the actions of the cruel wife who abandoned me."

"No one seriously buys that story."

"You'd think that. And yet, every day, I deal with someone offering me her bosom to cry on."

Natasha saw what he was doing, trying to make her jealous, only she wasn't about to fall victim to his games. "I'm glad you've got people to console you. It's important to have the right person, which is why I'm glad my father introduced me to Simon." She lay it on thick, and he bought it.

"I can't believe you're letting your family push you into marrying that asshole." The expletive spilled from his lips and showed her a chink in his armor.

Jealousy? It pleased her enough that she smiled and poked at that angry side of him. "Who says they're pushing? Have you seen him? Tall and handsome, quite accomplished, too. Finished top of his class in college."

Despite her attempt, he managed to stifle the jealous flare. "How lucky for you that your arranged marriage has turned into true love."

She almost blurted the truth: that she didn't love him. Probably never would. Simon didn't consume her thoughts. Didn't make every part of her vibrate with awareness.

"It's a good match." A solid one that would produce perfect little heirs.

"If you say so." His tone expressed his doubt, and she hated his astuteness. The reality was that the main reason she'd agreed to marry Simon was because she'd made a promise to her dying babushka. Funny how she could kill anyone the family told her to handle, but when her babushka told her she wished Natasha would marry that St. Petersburg heir and make some babies, she'd not argued—much. Mostly because her aunt Cecilia grabbed her in a headlock and yelled, "Promise her, you twit, she's dying." Which turned out to not be entirely accurate.

Babushka had a miraculous recovery not long after Natasha agreed to marry Simon, meaning she could still lord it over the family streak, which for the non-tiger-born meant queen bitch over the striped masses.

"Are you done with your questions regarding my upcoming nuptials?" she snapped. "I'd like to get done with our business."

"Say it like it is, baby. Divorce. Thing is, I don't think I want one. Doesn't seem right to just give up."

The gun ended up suddenly pointed at his face. "Either you sign the papers I've brought, or I shoot you. Your choice." She really hoped he didn't choose the latter. She didn't have a spare set of clothes if he ended up being a bloody squirter.

"You drive a hard bargain, baby."

"No bargain. It's do or die."

"Let's see those papers."

The gun remained trained on him while her other

hand pulled the envelope tucked into the long pocket stitched down her thigh. Cargo pants were her garment of choice when she went skydiving. The papers never cleared her pocket, her gaze instead caught by a red dot. She left the envelope in her pocket and instead watched the dot as it dragged and dipped rapidly across the wall, seeking a target.

There was a less than fifty percent chance it was for her. Didn't matter. She yelled, "Down."

The man didn't argue. He hit the floor, landing on his hands, gaze tilted to follow the red dot.

Natasha dropped to her haunches and spun to see out the glass window she'd smashed. Which, in retrospect, did scream *attention whore*. She'd thought about coming in the front, knocking like a mature adult, but... her way was more fun. She'd wanted to catch her supposed husband off guard.

Instead, the man, as suave as ever, acted as if he'd been expecting her.

The dot extinguished without a shot fired, but that didn't stop her from running in a half-crouch out the door, avoiding the shards of glass, gun held and ready to fire.

Emerging into the night, it took a moment to orient her senses.

His pool, lit from the lights embedded in the tile shell, illuminated the night in ripples. Shadows appeared to move, mostly because of the shifting water rippling the light. By the cabana, she noticed something out of place, a deeper pocket of black.

She ran for the spot of darkness, only to see a flash of fur tear by, orange and black, with a ridiculously fluffy mane and a tufted tail also in orange and black. The coloring of a tiger, with the fur of a lion. Neville had shifted into his tigon, and she stumbled at the sight.

He was ridiculous and gorgeous all at once. How had she never seen this side of him before? Their whirlwind courtship had never allowed the time for her to ever meet more than the man.

Rawr. He pounced, and something squeaked.

"Don't eat them!" she yelled. Not until she knew who they were aiming at. Probably her husband. No one knew she'd be here.

A sound at her back had her turning. Her gaze scanned the dim interior of the house before rising to the roofline. She'd knocked the sensors out on her way in, the helicopter being kind enough to let her drop a mile back. She'd coasted in using a short-term propulsion glider. It helped that the winds were in her favor tonight.

The roof had a visitor with a gun, the red spot of it aiming past her towards the scuffling and growling bodies.

"Oh no, you don't!" She ran for the patio table, leaping to the top of it and then springing again, fingers reaching for the roof's edge. She gripped the eavestrough and swung her legs to hook. In a second, she'd clambered onto the terra cotta tile and was racing after the quickly moving target.

They reached the peak and disappeared down the other side. In seconds, she was over the top in time to see them leaping. Then, *vroom*, the grumble of an engine as they took off, the single red taillight of the motorbike mocking her.

Ugh. She sat down on the edge of the roof and was just leaping down when a naked man came running from the side of the house, yelling, "Come back with my bike, asshole!"

Now it should be noted that a naked Neville was just as sexy as a naked Dean, changing his name in her mind didn't negate that fact. She'd never had any complaints about his body. Not even the striped fur on his chest. She knew for a fact that he dyed it on top to keep it dark. A dye that didn't survive the shift. His bright, striped hair was ruffled as he raked a hand through it, and he sounded quite disgruntled as he said, "Why didn't you shoot them?"

"I only shoot those that deserve it."

He cast her a glare. "You keep threatening to shoot me."

Her lips quirked. "Proving my point." She hopped to the ground. "Any reason why someone is trying to kill you?"

"Until tonight, no one was."

"I find that hard to believe."

He shrugged. "I'm not saying no one has ever tried. But they usually only get one shot."

"Arrogant."

"Not if it's true."

"Listen, I don't need to get involved in your problems. I just came for a divorce. Consider yourself served." She pulled the envelope with the documents and held them out, doing her best to keep her gaze on his face and not the naked body that tempted the eye.

He didn't grab the papers. "If you don't mind, I'm going to find some pants first. Then a drink. And after that, I'm going to question the person in my pool house."

She blinked at him. "You caught the shooter?"

"Not all of us failed." He stalked off, taut ass a thing to stare at, taking some of the sting out of his insult.

"The person I was chasing had a head start!" she argued, following that ass.

"And you were slow. Why didn't you shift?"

"Not all of us feel a need to do so in public."

"My yard isn't public."

"Tell that to your two visitors."

He paused and whirled to glare at her. "Are you really going to blame me for being a victim?"

Just because she knew it would irritate, she said, "Yes."

"I can see why the Tigranov streak chose you as their ambassador of evil."

She blinked. "My official job title is enforcer."

"Same thing."

"Sounds like you're jealous."

"Can you blame me?" he retorted. "Who wouldn't want to be a killer for hire for the most important people in our society?"

"A normal person."

He bared his teeth when he smiled and said, "Who says I'm normal?"

"How is it I never noticed this sarcastic side to you when we met before?" she asked with a frown.

"Because I liked you."

The meaning being clear: *I don't like you now.*

It shouldn't have made her sad.

As they rounded the house, the cabana now in view, she said, "You're one to talk about my job given you're not actually a chef but a killer for the Pride Group."

"Hunter," he corrected. "And I'm flattered you took the time to find out about me."

"I didn't...That is..." She stammered as she realized she'd admitted to having him researched. "Were you ever going to tell me?" was what she ended up blurting.

He shrugged. "Maybe. Given your timid nature, I was making sure you could handle my violent side before divulging it. At worst, my cover as a chef would have worked."

"What if I'd truly been that innocent little girl, and I'd run when I discovered the truth?"

No mistaking the feral nature of his grin when he said, "I would have chased."

The question being, what would he have done when he caught her?

The delicious shiver that went through her body had some fine ideas that had everything to do with pleasuring flesh and not torturing pain.

"You use your job as a cover," she stated.

"Being a renowned connoisseur of food, who likes his ingredients fresh, does come in handy for the tasks that take me away from my base city."

"It's a good cover," was her grudging reply.

As they traversed the pool deck, he cursed. "Shit." The cabana door gaped wide open.

"Apparently, you're a better chef than hunter. Looks like your catch is gone."

"Impossible! I had them tucked tighter than a boar for Christmas dinner on a spit over a coal fire."

For a moment, she could almost taste the crackling fat, and her mouth watered. "That's rather specific."

"Just mentioning the impossibility of the shooter getting loose."

"Maybe the wind blew the door open."

He entered the cabana and emerged shaking his head and holding on to a robe. "They're gone. Dammit." He shrugged on the robe and belted it. Shame. He had nothing to hide.

"For a big-time hunter, your security sucks." she taunted.

"Maybe I should hire a pro to fix it."

She arched her brow. "Don't look at me. I'm not available for work on account that I'm getting married in a week."

"That soon, huh?" He turned away from her, and her attention got caught by a solid red light peeking out of the flowerpot by the cabana door.

Had there always been a light? "Um, is that a camera by that hibiscus plant?"

He turned to follow her pointing finger, crouched, and parted the leaves. "Shit. Bomb. Take cover." He'd just thrown himself in her direction when the explosion hit.

CHAPTER FOUR

The impact of the bomb tossed him off his feet, and Dean flew right off the edge of the pool deck and into the water, which was better than over the cliff. Luckily, he hit the liquid in his human shape. His cat, being a bit of a pussy, was of the mind that if it didn't have bubbles and a ducky, then it was a waste of time.

He hit the water feet first and sank to the bottom, which gave him some protection against bullets and other projectiles that might harm his fleshy parts. Dean kept his eyes open and watched as best he could through the agitation as things plopped into the pool with him. Lawn chair, part of a table, chunks of siding from the cabana, an unconscious wife...

What a mess. He'd need a crew to come in and drain the pool, then clean it, not to mention rebuild his cabana, mundane tasks that he shoved to the back of his mind for more pressing matters.

1. Who the hell had sent snipers to his house armed with a bomb?
2. Were they after him or something else? And...
3. If he didn't do something to save Natasha, he'd end up a widower.

Oddly enough, despite her attitude, he found himself not keen on that idea. He began to kick across the pool, aiming for her plummeting body, only to stroke faster as her momentum slowed, and utterly relaxed, she began to float upward. This close, he could see her eyes shut and limbs hanging limply. He didn't spot any blood; however, he knew for a fact that sometimes the worst injuries didn't present any signs at all.

In more positive news, the exploding chunks ceased hitting the pool's surface, and it began to calm, making them targets. The latter being not so positive.

With a wary gaze for bullets trying to streak past the water barrier, he kicked and strained until he could reach out and grab Natasha, his fingers closing around her slender yet muscled arm. Months ago, he'd actually fallen for her story that the firm tone she kept her body in came from hot yoga.

Now, he knew better.

Holding tightly to her, Dean shoved to the surface, dragging her face into the evening air. His gaze bounced around, looking for movement, listening for signs of the enemy. But they'd already fled. Or so his instincts claimed.

He didn't relax, though, not until he heard Natasha take a breath. He kept hold as he stroked for the shallow end of the pool. Away from the shooting flames.

His cabana burned, and in the distance, he heard sirens. Nosy neighbors. There might be a few hundred yards between the properties, but as soon as he lit the barbecue—with a can of lighter fluid and enough charcoal to roast dozens of steaks—the firemen came tromping onto his property. Commending him on having not one but *two* fire extinguishers nearby, and then leaving with apologies—and bellies full of steak— not all that sorry for bothering him. Each time, his neighbor Frank woke to something having peed inside his house.

Might be time to get a new neighbor because it was inconvenient having human officials showing up so soon. They'd ask questions that he'd have a hard time answering—because the truth wasn't an option.

Exiting via the pool's shallow end stairs, Natasha's limp body in his arms, he strode straight into the house, moving as quickly as he dared with his wet feet on marble and hardwood. He didn't have time to do much, but he set a quick stage before the first of the firetrucks and policemen arrived on the scene.

By the time they ran into the backyard, trampling his gardens on their way, Dean was spraying at the flames with a garden hose, a cigar in his mouth, his wet shirt stinking of booze, his grin that of a partially drunk rich boy.

"Hallo there, officers." He saluted them with the hand holding the watering hose. The cops yelled as he sprayed them—not so accidentally. He held in a smirk as they jumped back.

"What's going on here?" barked the dark-skinned female officer with steel threading her black, curly hair. She wore a navy blue uniform and had her hand on the butt of her weapon. The name on her jacket read: *Beaumont*. Her gaze flicked between him and the flames at his back.

"Just having a late-night drink and a smoke." He winked and waved the cigar and the hose at the same time. This time, he didn't antagonize and spray anyone. While she remained by his side, the fire crew in yellow suspenders ran past, yanking a thick hose that made him wince. His poor lawn.

"We received reports of an explosion."

"Damned right, you did!" Dean exclaimed. He pointed with the water towards the back of the firemen battling the now diminished blaze. "That there bonfire is costing me a fortune. Who knew that old whiskey was so flammable?"

"You set this fire, sir?"

He smiled as he lied. "I did. But not on purpose. Do me a favor?" He lowered his voice and shot Officer Beaumont a conspiratorial look. "Don't tell my wife."

"Too late, you idiot!" Natasha strode out of the house, hair wrapped in a towel, wearing his robe, which while knee-length on him, reached to her ankles. "What have you done now?"

"Nothing," he said, ducking his head and tucking his hands behind his back, which led to more spraying water.

"Sir!" the female cop exclaimed.

"Oops." He shrugged as he let go of the hose nozzle handle, shutting off the stream.

"You were smoking and drinking again?" Natasha exclaimed, jabbing a finger at him. "I thought we talked about this! You're in rehab."

"It was just one cigar."

She tapped a foot and arched her brow.

"And maybe a glass or two of whiskey."

"My mother was right. I never should have married you!" she exclaimed.

"But, baby, I love you."

"If you loved me, you'd stay clean. But, no, you sneak out while I'm having a bath and this..."—she waved her hand—"this is what happens. I've had it." She stalked into the house, leaving him with a smirking police officer.

"I don't suppose you could go in there and claim it's arson?" he asked hopefully.

The woman snorted. "Are you asking me to lie?"

"I'm going to guess that's a no." He did his best to sound dejected about it, but in reality, that had gone better than hoped.

The scene was set. The fabricated truth more believable than reality. The officer never thought to wonder how a bottle of exploding booze caused so much damage. Never thought to ask why his wife took such a late bath at night, or how he'd gotten his hands on the whiskey he wasn't supposed to have.

It took longer than he liked to have them put out the fire and leave his property, but once they did... Dean was alone with his wife, in a robe, in the parlor, with no gun, but a candlestick.

Murder or seduction...it could go either way.

CHAPTER FIVE

Natasha pretended to smile and chide her husband while the fire was put out, and the officer wrote a report.

It took forever for them to leave.

Forever before she could turn around and glare at the man who happened to be her husband.

Someone who'd almost died. A good thing he hadn't since he'd saved her life.

How had she gone from planning to possibly kill him, to preventing a sniper from shooting him? It would have been much simpler to let a stranger handle her problem. Now, she had to deal with him and his annoying, jovial attitude.

"I don't know about you, but I could use a change of clothes and a drink. Actually, I think a hot shower is called for. Care to join me?" His grin had a bit of alley cat in it.

"No, I do not want to join you. I want answers."

"To what? The answer to life? I think Douglas Adam answered that in *The Hitchhiker's Guide to the Galaxy.*"

She couldn't help but blink at the inane answer. When she didn't reply, he continued. "It's forty-two, by the way."

"How is a number the answer to life?"

He shrugged. "You'd have to ask the computer that came up with it. But I'd have to assume it was accurate given it took him several million years to figure out."

"A fictional computer from a fictional story?"

"You know what they say, all stories, even the most unbelievable, have a kernel of truth in them."

"You know the tales you hear about how bad the Russian mob is?" she replied with an arched brow. "All true, and actually tamer than the reality."

"Guess it's a good thing I'm married to the mob, then." He winked.

"We are not married," she declared as if that would make all the difference.

"You say that, and yet we were the perfect image of a bickering couple for that cop. I have to say, the part where you told me I'd be sleeping on the couch was perfection." He kissed the tips of his fingers, and a shiver ran through her.

She'd not forgotten how those lips felt on her skin.

"You're cold. We should go back inside and take

that hot shower I was talking about. After you." He swept a bow.

"I don't want a shower."

"You say that now, but what if I promised to scrub your back?"

"Touch me, and I'll drown you."

"Testy tonight. They say our moods are closely connected to our sexual energy. Is Simon not doing it for you?" he asked as he headed into the house.

"My sex life is none of your business."

"On the contrary, wife, I am very interested in it." He stopped short just inside the room, and she had to wonder how the cop hadn't noticed the broken door. Then again, Neville had done a good job of sweeping the broken bits out of plain sight and drawing the blinds.

"Would you feel better if I said I orgasm on a regularly?"

"Masturbation, while healthy, isn't a substitute for a flesh on flesh climax. Would you like me to show you the difference?" His grin was wicked as he offered, and worse, she was tempted.

"Can you stop screwing around for just a minute?" she huffed. "Rather than worry about my sex life, we should be discussing why someone just tried to kill you." Later, she'd examine why she even gave a damn.

He cast her a glance over his shoulder as he walked across the sunroom. "What makes you so sure they were after me?"

"No one knew I was coming here."

"Maybe you were followed."

"Now, you're just being silly. Nobody would dare come after me." She had a family that would make death seem like a mercy compared to the alternative. Her papa wasn't the kind to forgive, especially anyone who hurt his daughter.

"I could say the same. Why come after me? Killing me would start a shitstorm of epic proportion."

"Arrogant much?"

"Always. But that said, I probably do have a string of enemies. And I'll bet you do, too."

"I was taught to never leave someone alive if they might do me harm," was her pert reply.

"Everyone has the potential to hurt, so how do you decide which of them lives?" he queried.

"Are you really discussing theology with me?"

"Why not? I thought I knew you once before. Apparently, I wasn't asking the right questions," he stated, letting the damp shirt reeking of booze slide from his broad shoulders.

"You want to know what kind of person I am?" Her tone lilted. "Fine. I am the kind who doesn't show mercy if you hurt me."

"That's pretty standard for most people."

"I can also be merciless if I don't like you."

"That's pretty broad. I mean, what if it's a random act that gets a person on your radar? For example, a person cuts you off in traffic and almost causes a crash." He tossed the ruined shirt into a garbage pail, cleverly hidden within his living room.

"I don't care if they're strangers. Do me wrong, and I will take note of the license plate, and pay a visit to slash some tires later." She also sometimes took a bat to their windshield. People who couldn't drive shouldn't have a car.

"I never knew you suffered from road rage."

"Because I always let you drive." At the time, he would have been stunned to hear the language that emerged from her when she got behind the wheel of a car.

"Anything else I should know about you that might not be documented?"

"How about the fact that I'll stab you with a fork if you touch my cheesecake."

"Really?" He arched a brow. Rakish to the extreme. "Way to make me crave some."

"Can we stop the idle chitchat? We have bombs and assassins to discuss."

"You were the one who got off track."

She couldn't have said if that were true or false because, quite honestly, she kept finding herself distracted by his bare chest. The smooth flesh showed the fine musculature she recalled. Not to mention the narrowing of his torso at his hips, and the taut ass showcased by his snug swim shorts.

"Do you know who wants to kill you?"

"Do you know who wants to kill *you*?" he parried.

"You, for one."

"Wrong, dear wife. If I wanted to be a widower, I'd have already rid myself of you."

"I'm not that easy to kill."

"Only because I haven't tried," he boasted.

"Would you really snuff me?" She batted her lashes.

His smile was deadly and devilishly handsome all at once as he said, "Like you, wrong me once, shame on me. I don't do second chances."

"I wronged you." She wouldn't start pretending that she hadn't.

"You did. And yet, I let you live, baby. Have you wondered why?"

"No." Because it had never actually occurred to Natasha that he'd try to harm her. Not the man she'd known. If briefly. And falsely. Even now, she didn't believe he'd do it. "You won't kill me."

"I think that's the truest thing to ever come out of your mouth."

"Are you going to whine again about the fact that I bested you?"

"Oh, you had me, all right. By the dick and balls. I quite enjoyed it. Let me know if you want to relive those moments." He winked.

She wanted to—take him up on his offer. But she wouldn't. She had a duty to perform.

"Let's go back to the assailants."

"Changing the subject? Is it getting uncomfortable?"

She chose not to answer. "In the time you were tying up your target, did you get any clues at all as to their identity? Who they might work for?"

"I didn't have time to question because the moment I tied them up turkey-style, I went looking for you. Just in time to save that pert ass."

He thought it pert? She wouldn't be distracted by such a ridiculous compliment. It would make her too girly. "I didn't need your help. I can handle myself. You should have done a better job with your target. Because of your shoddy knots, we lost your guy."

"Girl, as a matter of fact. Aren't you the sexist?" he taunted.

She glared. "*Guy* is unisex."

"Not in the context you used it."

He was right, but she wouldn't admit it. "Back to the girl you didn't tie very well—"

"I tied her quite nicely, I'll have you know. I am quite adept when it comes to knots."

"So am I. And when I tie up a guy, he doesn't get loose until I'm done with him." She made it sound dirty and was rewarded with a nostril flare.

He turned from her as he said in a tight voice, "Why, baby, I never knew you were into those kinds of games. Maybe I should have spanked you after the wedding for being a naughty girl."

"Lay a hand on my ass, and I'll break it."

"Tempting," he drawled, turning from a sideboard with a drink in hand. He held it out to her. "Scotch? I'm afraid I'm out of vodka."

"I don't need a drink. I want to know about the woman who escaped. Can you describe her?"

He tossed back the alcohol first. "She was shorter than you. Thicker. Heavier."

"What color was her hair?"

"No idea."

"Eyes? Skin?"

He shrugged. "She wore a hoodie. I only got the quickest of glimpses before I left to find you."

"Ugh." Natasha paced. "That doesn't help at all."

"Are you planning to hunt her down? I'm surprised you'd care. Didn't you say being a widow would solve your problems?"

It would, and yet if he died, it should be by her hand, on her terms. "If someone is trying to kill you, I want to know why."

"Why, baby, I knew you cared." He beamed as he saluted her with his glass.

She scowled, mostly because she knew he taunted her. "I don't give a damn about you. I'm more interested in making sure this attempt isn't connected to my family or me."

"Ouch. Very cold, baby."

"Would you stop that? I am not your baby."

"But you are my wife until I sign those papers.

Which are gone, by the way. They didn't survive the dunking."

"Where are my clothes?" She'd woken naked and under the covers of his bed, her sodden clothes out of sight. It wasn't hard to find an oversized t-shirt and robe to wear down the stairs when she faked the part of his wife.

Only she didn't have to fake much. They actually were married. It still hadn't quite sunken in.

"Your stuff went down the laundry chute. I didn't have time to throw them in the washer before the company arrived."

"You do realize the cops have you pegged as an alcoholic rich boy?"

"Yes."

"Nice cover," she added begrudgingly and not without admiration. He'd hidden in plain sight and masked his actions as debauched partying.

"Your social persona is pretty good, too."

"Don't you mean perfect? I am exactly as I seem. A spoiled rich girl with a doting papa."

Half his mouth lifted. "Who kills people who wrong her family."

She shrugged. "It's how I was raised." Her papa had instilled a strong sense of family in her, maybe too much after her mother had died. Some would call her father a mean bastard. Maybe to outsiders. But he adored his little girl.

"I need clothes," she said, looking down at the dark blue robe.

"Don't tell me you didn't bring a spare set." He snorted. The implication being that she should have thought ahead. In her defense, she hadn't expected to go for a swim.

"I came in light."

"Good thing for you, I have some stuff that might fit." A room full to be exact. Women's clothing in all kinds of styles and sizes.

She couldn't help a tart, "Entertain much?"

"Yes," he growled. "Damned Pride biatches think they can come over whenever they like."

She bristled. "With that kind of attitude, I'm surprised they haven't slit your throat."

"Why would they cut it when they love me?" he said mournfully. "Apparently, my saying '*no*' is playing hard to get. So, they keep coming over. Bringing me food. Leaving their stuff. Sometimes, trying to crawl into my bed when I'm asleep."

She stiffened, unable to halt the hot flood of jealousy. "I'm sure you hate all that attention."

"I like sleeping alone. And, as a chef, I cannot condone the eating of those gelatin and whipped cream desserts they keep bringing. If they truly wanted to win my heart, they should try making homemade pasta and sauce, or a roast with all the trimmings." He sounded mournful.

She set him straight. "I don't cook."

"A good thing I can. Does this mean you'll handle all the grocery shopping, then?"""

Her mouth rounded into an O of surprise. "No."

"What about house cleaning? Should we engage a maid, or would you like us to make up a chore list? You take care of the garbage, vacuuming, and mopping, I'll handle the dishes and the toilets."

"What are you doing?"

"Making sure divorce is the right choice. I mean, what if we're being hasty and we're a perfect match?" He smiled.

Natasha scowled in reply. "We are getting divorced."

"Maybe."

She almost threw herself at him. He wouldn't grin so smugly when she punched him in the mouth a few times. She hated to lose. Just ask Cousin Ivan, who never again looked her in the eye after the time he'd bragged that he'd gotten to the boss level in the game they were both playing. He also never played video games again.

Dressing in various odds and ends, she noted the time. Not quite morning, but well past a proper bedtime.

Maybe she'd head to her temporary home, grab a few hours of sleep, get another copy of the divorce papers and... Hold on. That involved leaving Neville Horatio Fitzpatrick alone. On his own. With two potential assassins on the loose, maybe more—and women who thought they could just pop in and seduce her husband.

She eyed him. "You're going to have to come with me."

"Are you going somewhere?"

"Yes, and given I need your signature, you are coming, too."

"I'm tired. The only place I'm going is to bed."

He headed away from her and down the hall, she knew this because she followed.

"You can't seriously be thinking of staying here."

"Why not?"

"For one, the broken sliding glass door."

"That exploding whiskey bottle sure made a mess." The explanation given to the police officer.

"It's not safe here."

"Says you. I feel perfectly fine." He flopped onto his bed, a waterbed she noted that wobbled when he landed.

Having located not only a knife but a gun while browsing the garments, she felt no compunction in firing a bullet into his mattress.

Kersplash.

She stood just out of reach of the resulting flood. The man, lying within the soggy frame, sighed heavily. "You win. Take me to your boudoir since you insist."

"It's a friend's home."

"Even more sordid. Shall we be sharing a couch?

Because if that's the case, I'd really rather we just rent a room."

"Since when are you such a princess?"

"I wouldn't talk, baby. According to the gossip mill, you have champagne tastes and throw a tantrum when they're not met."

She rolled a shoulder coyly. "You're not the only one who can play dilettante." Did he know how much he revealed when he admitted that he'd followed her online? Just how much about her did he know? If he had sources as good as hers, then that could be quite a bit.

Or he was playing her because anyone who truly knew her reputation wouldn't be so blasé.

"Speaking of which." He suddenly held up a phone and snapped a picture of her.

"What are you doing?" she squeaked, conscious of the fact that she wore a towel on her head. "Delete that at once."

"Too late. Already posted."

"Where? You idiot. You'd better get rid of it before anyone sees it."

"Does it really matter?" he asked.

"I'm supposed to be in Europe, on my way to Italy for my bachelorette."

His expression brightened. "Hell, yeah. You know this means I get a bachelor party, too. With strippers."

Her finger twitched, and she was tempted to throw

something at him. "You're not the one getting married."

"Because I already am. So, if you get to have a party after the fact, so do I. Or did you want to go modern and combine it into a Jack and Jill?"

"We are getting divorced," she hissed as he kept up the annoying pretense that they should make their marriage work.

"Says you. Hasn't happened yet, and until we do, I'm getting everything I can out of the arrangement. Which means a bachelor party with my closest buds, getting drunk, listening to horror stories of the ball and chain, and stuffing bills down some g-strings."

"Sounds sexist and degrading to women."

"Oh, really, and what do you have planned for your party, little miss likes to get drunk and post selfies where your lips look like you've gotten punched they're pursed so far? I'm going to wager something pretty damned close to mine."

She hated that he was right. "It's a sham for the public me."

"Because we wouldn't want the world to know you're actually an intelligent, accomplished woman."

Danger. His words had a seductive brilliance to them that managed to wind themselves around her, warming her. She held strong against the allure. "I don't need validation from outsiders to know my worth."

"And what are you worth, baby?"

"As if you can pin a number on me." She lifted her chin. "I'm priceless."

"Exactly. And yet you expect me to walk away. What if I don't want to?"

He kept insisting on making the marriage work, and she wouldn't completely lie and say that she wasn't tempted. Except she knew one thing: he wouldn't survive a week. Her family would never allow it.

"It's not about what you want." It was the closest thing to the truth she could give him. In some respects, it wasn't about her wants, either. "Now, if you're done wasting time, can we get out of here?"

"What's wrong, baby? Can't handle me wet?" He winked as he rose from the shallow puddle of his bed, skin moist, tempting, lickable.

Hard... Her gaze strayed down, and he uttered a small rumble as he strode past her to the closet. Stripping off his shorts and giving her a peek of his taut ass before it disappeared into the walk-in.

"Give me a second to dress and pack a bag."

She stood waiting less than patiently until he emerged with a satchel, wearing low-slung track pants, slip-on loafers, and nothing else.

"Where's your shirt?" she asked.

"In the bag."

"Shouldn't you be wearing it?" He really should cover up so she didn't keep staring.

"Given your haste in trying to get me away from

here to your den of iniquity, I assume I won't be wearing it long. No point in ruining a good shirt."

"I want to leave so we can get to my crash pad and sleep."

"Of course, you want to *sleep*." He said it in a way that implied anything but and added finger quotes.

"We are. In separate beds."

"Oh, good. Because you steal blankets."

"I do not!" she huffed.

"Says the woman who would caterpillar into it every night, leaving me freezing."

"There's grounds for divorce right there," she declared.

"Seems a little drastic. Why not just raise the thermostat so I'm not chilly? Or I could snuggle you for warmth." He arched a brow.

"Stop it," she snapped, stomping to his front door.

"Stop what?" said with the innocence of a brat with his hand caught in the cookie jar.

"I know what you're doing. And it won't work."

"Are you sure of that?" he purred quickly by her ear, the vibration of the words on her lobe before he opened a door leading into an attached garage. He cast her a glance. "Shall we take the Benz?"

"Only if I drive."

He reached inside the open door and returned with some keys. "Catch."

Her fingers curled around the plastic fob. He'd soon regret that choice. As they left his property, she laughed as she took the curves at the highest speed the car could handle.

To her surprise, rather than looking pale, she glanced over to see the jerk smiling, the picture of poised relaxation.

Would he never cease to surprise her?

She couldn't help but compare him to her current fiancé. A sop of a fellow, handsome enough in a blond, perfectly coiffed and yuppy kind of way. It was a marriage of convenience and power, the joining of two powerful families.

A way for her to branch out from under her family's thumb.

If Simon misbehaved, accidents happened. Her papa and grandmother knew she wouldn't tolerate disrespect. Not that she worried about that with Simon. Truthfully, he wasn't all that bad. Boring, yes, blander than dry bran cereal, but he was kind to her, courteous, sending her cards and flowers at the oddest moments. Romantic gestures that seemed strange given he'd yet to even kiss her. Then again, they weren't often alone together. The occasions they were proved to be for the press. Her babushka was the one who'd taught her how to focus the media's eye on one thing to draw attention away from others.

The drive wasn't a bad one, twenty minutes and she was pulling into the large, circular driveway that peaked at the front of a three-story house.

Her temporary husband stared at the place and said, "I can't stay here. Let's find a hotel instead."

"And piss off my uncle, Vinny." She snorted. "Not likely. Let's go." She exited the car, and he slowly followed, only to freeze at the doorway that opened when she placed her hand on the screen, which lit up as it scanned her prints.

"Trust me when I say I really shouldn't stay," he repeated.

"Are you scared of my uncle? I swear, he's only half as bad as they claim." Which depending on who was telling the stories, was pretty bad.

"I'm not worried about Vinny. It's his dau—"

"Dean!" The squeal emerged from the top of the stairs, high-pitched and excited. And then her cousin Isabella was flying down the steps, her feet barely touching the floor, wearing a skimpy pair of shorts, a tiny tank top, and nothing under them.

It didn't take seeing Neville's expression to realize he was familiar with her cousin. Too familiar.

Isabella hit the bottom step and tossed herself at him, and he didn't even have the courtesy to stagger when she hit him. Nor did he drop her, which might have had to do with the fact that Isabella anaconda-ed his ass with her arms and legs.

"Dean," she squealed again. "It's been so long since I've seen you."

"Hello, Isa, it's nice to see you, too," Neville

replied to the squirming, happy bundle of dark curls and pretty features bouncing against him.

"Why are you here? You should have called me. I must look like a mess," Isabella declared. Having seen Isabella all decked out, Natasha could state with confidence that she was stupidly gorgeous both ways.

"Funny coincidence, I actually live in the next town over. Got a place on the cliffs."

"Nice. Why didn't you tell me you'd moved into the area?" She playfully slapped his arm, and Natasha tucked her hands behind her back before she knocked her cousin out.

"I wasn't sure if I should. As you said, it's been a while." Neville set Isabella down on her feet, not that it stopped her from beaming at him, and cocking a hip that only drew attention to the satin shorts and thin top clinging to her breasts. Someone give the girl a sweater. Judging by her protruding nips, she was cold.

"So, how come you're here? Did Tasha bring you?" Isabella asked, using a family nickname.

"Actually, she did. There's been a slight mishap at my place, and she was kind enough to offer me a place to sleep for the night."

"Tasha did?" Isabella gaped at her, and she could see all the different scenarios running through her cousin's head.

"It's just for one night," she grumbled.

"Or more if he needs," Isabella immediately offered. "What happened to your house?"

"Assassins." He shrugged nonchalantly as if it were an everyday thing. It only served to round Isabella's eyes and heighten her interest.

"How utterly dangerous," she cooed. "Do you think they'll follow you here?"

"Possibly."

Before Isabella could run off and wake her uncle, Natasha interceded. "He's exaggerating. It's not that bad. His pool house caught fire, and his place smells smoky."

"There's also a bullet hole in my waterbed," he confided. "Apparently, my wife didn't approve of my choice."

"Wife? Who?" Isabella squeaked.

He'd better not. He'd—

He smiled and said, "Your cousin."

Natasha wanted to kill him. Her family didn't know about her shameful secret. She'd hoped to handle it quietly and had only told her uncle because he had the best lawyer to handle it.

"You're married?" Isabella squeaked. "To her?" She couldn't have sounded more horrified if she tried. Isabella's eyes rounded.

"Yes, although we have gotten off to a rocky start. A bit of a misunderstanding. But now that we're together again, I'm hoping to reconcile," he blabbed.

"Never," Natasha huffed.

"I swear, I didn't know," Isabella lifted her hands and backed away from him.

"No need to apologize. We're getting divorced," she snapped. "The wedding was an accident."

"Maybe, and yet it still counts," he taunted.

"Don't make her mad," exclaimed Isabella, who had a healthy respect for cousin Natasha, who'd once shaved her bald for calling her a rude name.

"Why not? She's got the prettiest eyes when she's pissed," Neville declared while ducking as Natasha swung for him.

"I should have shot you!" she yelled. "It's not too late." She pulled a gun, but before she could aim, he knocked it from her hand, and it hit the floor with a clatter.

"I think I should leave now." Isabella backed away from them as if they carried the plague.

"Not yet, you aren't," Natasha growled. "How do you know Neville?" she asked, snapping her fingers when Isabella didn't immediately reply.

"Who's Neville?"

"Dean. His real name is Neville. How do you know him?"

"It was a long time ago. Years. In college."

"We were both students. We met at a frat party," he added. "We were so wasted that first night."

Isabella shot him a glare before she fluttered her hands. "It was a long time ago. It meant nothing."

"Explain...nothing." Her tone was flat. Meanwhile, jealousy raged inside.

Her cousin turned a pasty shade of cement. "We dated for a little while."

"Dated?" Neville purred. "We did a lot more than just hold hands at the movies. You brought me home to meet your father for Christmas."

"You were an actual couple?" The jealousy did more than bubble, it had Natasha digging her nails into her palms. A good thing he'd knocked the gun away, or she might have shot her cousin.

"We hooked up for what? Six, seven months?" he declared. "In the end, we just weren't the right fit."

"Not even close." Isabella rolled on the balls of her feet. "And it happened ages ago."

"You looked awfully happy to see him," Natasha remarked in a flat tone.

Isabella swallowed and squeaked. "I think I should go now."

"Yes, you should. Run along, *Isa*." She enunciated the shortened name and nothing else, yet her cousin bolted back up those stairs as if a pack of hyenas chased her.

Neville chided her. "Did you have to scare her like that?"

She narrowed her gaze on him. Why was he trying to protect her? Did he still have feelings for Isa? "Not my fault she's skittish. I wouldn't have had to say anything at all if you'd kept your mouth shut."

"I'm not the one ashamed of the fact that we got married."

"For the last time, it was supposed to be fake," she growled, stomping away from him and heading for the kitchen. She could use something to eat.

He kept pace. "Why the complicated charade, though? That's the part I can't figure out. Use me to get close to Lawrence, I get that. But you didn't need to pretend we were getting married. You bought a dress. Made it to the end of the ceremony before making your move."

She wasn't about to admit that hadn't originally been part of the plan. However, the ritual started, and Dean had looked at her so lovingly, she'd not been able to resist playing along in the fantasy for a moment before she shattered it.

"I wasn't sure what would bring your friend Lawrence out of hiding. I did think about kidnapping you and holding you as a hostage for an exchange. But that might have caused problems with the Pride. The lion king is fond of you."

"We go way back," he admitted. Their mothers used to hang out a few times a month at a protected park where rambunctious boys could run and tumble.

"Which left me with marriage. After all, what kind of best friend doesn't show up to a wedding?"

"Would you have really killed him over jilting your cousin?"

"I once killed a guy for taking the last cherry-filled donut at the store when I had a craving." And it had been worth every powdered-sugared, sweet, gelatinous bite.

"I guess I should be honored then that you haven't killed me."

"You should be."

"Since it means you like me."

"I do not. Did you not hear me before when I said I didn't want to start a war with your king?"

"Please. As if you'd leave any evidence linking you or your family to my demise."

"I'd probably plant the blame on someone else," she admitted, like those damned Russian bears who thought they could home in on their business.

"It's okay to admit you like me," he confided with a wink. "I'm just that kind of guy."

"The kind that makes me want to commit unspeakable acts of violence, you mean?" she said, opening the refrigerator and seeing a wrapped container with meat inside. To her surprise, he joined her in the fridge, pulling out the fixings for a sandwich.

If she ignored the jam.

Except when he slathered it on one sandwich then offered the knife, she had to ask, "Why would you put raspberries on a roast beef sandwich?"

"Sweet and salty, baby. Give it a try." He held out his idea of a sandwich masterpiece, and she hesitated before taking a bite.

Her eyes widened as she chewed. "That's actually not bad."

"Please, we both know it is delicious. I got the idea after making leftover Thanksgiving sandwiches with cranberries. It's all about complementing flavors," he claimed before devouring his sandwich. He said not a word as she slathered jam on hers and then chowed down, too.

As they sat in companionable if chewing silence, she couldn't help peeking at Neville. This man was the same one she'd met months ago, and not at the same time. This version proved more open, more sarcastic and outrageous.

More...himself.

It shouldn't have made him more attractive, and yet, it did. He brimmed with vitality and arrogance. She didn't doubt for a minute he'd meant it when he said that he'd rather stay married. He was stubborn and confident. A pity he wasn't a full-blooded tiger. Knowing what her family was capable of, there was no point in even trying.

"You are so lucky to have an Uncle Vinny," he declared after he'd downed his glass of milk."

"Because of the movie?"

"No, because I hear he throws the best Halloween parties."

"He does. Full-sized candy bars and pop. Bobbing for apples. The haunted maze he has built in the front yard is epic."

"Did you grow up around here?" he asked.

"No, but my papa brought me often to visit. Said it

was important that I have a connection to Mama's family."

"Your mother died when you were young."

She pushed at her plate. "Yes." She didn't like to talk about it.

"Want to hear something messed up?"

"What?" she asked.

"When I was doing my digging on your family, I discovered that my dad dated your mother."

She blinked. "Are we related?"

He grinned. "Not that anyone is admitting."

"Bastard."

"If it helps, my parents were married a year before they had me. But on that same note, I never did have any genetic tests done, so we could be brother and sister."

"Really revising my plan to kill you."

"Your bloodthirsty nature makes me wonder if they had you watching *The Godfather* from the cradle. You really take your role as mob princess quite seriously."

"Stop calling me that."

"No princess. No baby. No wife. I'm running out of things to call you."

"How about Natasha?"

"After all we've been through? I deserve something more intimate than that."

"You're going to earn my foot up your ass if you keep irritating me."

"You were the one who insisted I stick with you. I was perfectly happy to stay at home in my bed. Speaking of which, where am I sleeping?"

There were plenty of empty rooms. Rooms with a bed he could use, out of sight.

"You'll stay with me." She had a king-size. Surely, it would provide enough space.

"Afraid I'll sneak off in the middle of the night?"

More like she worried someone might sneak in, and she wasn't just thinking about the assassins.

She grabbed a glass of milk that she'd warmed in the microwave and led the way. He said nothing as he entered the suite her uncle had loaned her. She kept her back to him as she chugged the warm beverage. It always soothed her nerves—even as a child.

When she crawled into bed, it was to find him already lying on the covers on the other side.

More than enough space for the two of them.

So why did she end up splayed across his very naked chest late the next morning?

CHAPTER SIX

The moment Natasha became aware of her position, she stiffened. As she squirmed, Dean stiffened too, albeit for a different reason.

"Morning, baby," he drawled.

"Mauling me in my sleep?" she declared, but rather than slink away, she remained lying atop him.

"Nice try, princess. But you were the one to climb on top of me and make little noises of protest if I so much as shifted a muscle to get comfortable."

"You're built like a rock," she mumbled, only to stammer. "And are thick like one, too. I mean..."

"No need to explain. I am very much aware of how thick and solid I am."

The innuendo had her groaning.

"Make that sound again," he grumbled.

She ducked her face against him, and her warm

breath tickled the skin over his ribs. "We need to get up."

"I already am." He was deliberate in his word choice.

She made him pay. She rose up from under the blankets wearing only a long shirt and panties, and fully straddled him. A thigh on either side, her groin pressed against him, a hot, moist mess even with her underthings. A goddess with hair tangled and tumbling down her back.

"I think you need to pee," she declared, giving him a firm rub. "But I'm going first!" Then she was gone, pert ass peeking from her high-cut undies.

His dick throbbed something fierce. Not with urine, he should add.

He didn't have time to fix the problem. She'd be back any second now.

Or not.

She stayed in that bathroom long enough that he worried she'd drowned in the toilet. When she opened the door, she looked entirely too smug, and not one bit horny.

More like the cat that got into the cream.

"You masturbated!" he accused boldly.

Her reply emerged even bolder as she lifted her chin and said, "Twice."

He really wished he'd fisted himself and spewed his seed onto her pillow. Instead, his balls ached.

Unfair. But he wasn't about to emasculate himself with the admission.

"I'm surprised you didn't bring a phone in there with you so you could share the pleasure with your fiancé."

"Who needs a phone when there's built-in video calling." She sauntered out, wearing a towel and nothing else.

Hot anger filled him at the thought she might have given a show to another man. How dare she cheat on him?

Then again, knowing her as he did, he had to wonder. He relaxed, arm under his head. "How is Simon? Have you told him yet that you're already married?"

"Actually, I told him I missed him and couldn't wait to be his wife." She walked into the closet, and he lay back, closing his eyes.

He would not go on a rampage. He would not hunt this Simon down and strip the skin from his bones. He wouldn't let her get under his fur. But for that to happen, he needed to start controlling the situation.

What could he do to regain the upper hand? How to throw her off balance enough for that mask she wore to slip?

The idea he got brought a smile to his lips.

When she emerged from the closet, she squeaked. "What are you doing?"

"Masturbating." Or so he made it seem under the

blankets, bumping his fist up and down in the groin area. Who would have thought someone as jaded as she could still blush?

He must have been convincing because she turned her back. "Can't you be discreet?"

"I'm under the blankets."

"I can see it moving."

"It?" He snorted.

"Sorry, would you prefer I call it your little soldier?"

He almost flung back the blanket to remind her of his true girth. He didn't, mostly because she still had a red flush to her cheeks. She remembered how well he was built.

"I don't suppose you want to come over here and do your wifely duty?" He tucked his hands behind his head.

"I won't be your wife for long."

She headed to the bureau and opened a laptop sitting atop it. In a moment, the portable printer she'd hooked up to a port spewed out several sheets.

She brought the sheaf over along with a pen and held them out. "Sign."

He thought about batting it down, but he had a better idea. He took the contract and ignored her to peruse it. The document appeared very simple and straightforward. A divorce with no strings, only he liked batting at things. "This won't do."

"Why not?"

"Because you forgot a few things."

Her brow furrowed. "Like?"

"Splitting of our property."

"You keep what you have. I keep my stuff."

"What about our friends?"

"We have no friends in common," she reminded.

"What about income?"

"Why does income matter?"

"Alimony, of course. Whoever makes more pays it."

"You can't be serious."

"Deadly serious. I married you with good intent. I'd say that's worth something."

Her mouth rounded. "You expect me to pay you."

When her hand suddenly moved, pulling forth a gun she'd tucked at the small of her back, he moved, avoiding the path of the bullet. The pillow he lay on didn't fare as well. Feathers floated in the air.

She fired again even as he was diving forward, staying low to the ground. The third one grazed him before he tossed himself forward.

Before she could aim again, he'd snared her ankles and thrown her off balance. She hit the floor on her ass, jostling her, giving him the time needed to grab her wrist and hold her gun-toting hand immobile. He didn't fool himself into thinking her tamed.

"I am not giving you a cent," she hissed, spitting mad, and gorgeous.

"Then I'm not giving you a divorce," he replied, yanking her close. "Wife."

"Don't call me that."

"But that's who you are. You're *my* wife." The word held a hint of a growl.

Her eyes dilated, and her breathing grew shallow. "I'm going to marry Simon."

"Over my dead body."

"If you insist."

The knife prodded at his belly.

He didn't care. He kissed her.

CHAPTER SEVEN

The touch of his mouth didn't ignite anything because she was already on fire. The sensual slide of his lips only served to bring the heat inside her to a boil.

And then it was over.

"Thank you for not biting off my lip," he said, pulling away.

"I was waiting for some tongue to do the most damage." She licked her lips, and his gaze followed. It did nothing to ease the need inside her. She might have masturbated, but that tiny orgasm wasn't what she really wanted. Not what she needed.

"You always did like to French kiss. But as I recall, you preferred my tongue licking another part of your body."

She sucked in a breath because she did remember.

How dare he. Of course, he dared because he could. The man she'd met as Dean always managed to throw her off balance. The only man to do so.

Ever.

Which made it strange that she'd not killed him yet. He certainly deserved it for plaguing her. Knowing they were married and yet ignoring her.

Staying far away.

Not once trying to contact her.

Never asked for a divorce either, and she had to wonder about his claims that he'd cheated.

She'd been watching. Not personally, of course. But she had her ways.

According to surveillance, he'd not been with another man or woman. Nothing that could be proven at any rate. However, there were lapses of time where her reports had nothing to say, where he'd dropped out of sight. He could have been doing anything. Doing someone.

The very idea made her blood boil. What did it mean? She'd not pursued it or allowed herself to truly wonder. Until now.

Face to face with him, she remembered why she'd lasted the whole wedding before ruining what they had. He still drew her more strongly than the cheesecake in the fridge that Chef made fluffy sweet.

Her accidental husband was more addictive than the catnip her babushka had cultivated. On a full moon, it was recommended to not peek out any of the windows overlooking the garden as Grandmother tended to enjoy it still with her paramour of the moment. In dishabille.

Eye bleach worthy at best.

"Cat got your tongue?" he teased, still gripping her wrist. She could have broken free. Could have hurt him, or even killed him and done away with the need for a divorce.

He knew it, too. Knew what she was.

Meaning he intentionally goaded her with his demand that they remain together. It wasn't about money, he had plenty. So, why?

She swayed against him, softening her stance and expression. "Perhaps instead of a divorce, you're right. We could reconcile. Give it a second chance."

He stiffened, not just his posture.

"Kiss and make up?"

The word *kiss* brought her gaze to his lips. Before his embrace, she'd wondered if her mind had inflated her memory of the pleasure. It had been so long...Yet it proved better than she recalled. And if a kiss was better—

She yanked free, bolted to her feet, and spun away from him, annoyed she'd so easily fallen for his tricks.

"We can't be doing this."

"Why not? We're married. We can do anything we like together."

"We can't be married, though. Don't you see?"

"Because you want to be married to that sop, Simon." He couldn't stop the angry downturn of his lips.

"I don't have a choice."

"Call it off."

"I can't. I've already agreed."

"You made me a promise first."

"Under false pretenses," she snapped.

"False for you, maybe. But it was real for me."

"So real, you let me go." Too late, the words slipped from her, revealing more than she intended. Bastard caught it.

"Are you upset I didn't chase after you?"

"No." Please don't let him hear the uncertainty in that reply.

"I thought about it, you know, especially at first when I was angry."

"Why didn't you come for me?" she asked.

He shrugged. "I'm not the type to chase after a woman."

"Just the type to be difficult when it comes to splitting up," she retorted.

"I don't easily give up what's mine."

"I don't belong to you," she hastily replied, even as her heart raced faster. There was something possessive in the way he said it that appealed to her baser instincts.

She was a strong, independent woman, but having

him try and dominate gave her a certain thrill.

"Are you sure about that, baby? It's been a while since I've licked you. Perhaps I should remind you what it's like to be with me." He eyed her mouth.

She hoped he couldn't smell her arousal. "Don't look at me like that."

"Like what?" he asked, looming over her. Making her realize how petite she was beside him.

Yet his size didn't daunt her. A part of her believed he'd never hurt her. On the contrary, she had a suspicion that he'd kill anyone who tried.

"You keep eyeballing me like I'm a delicious meal you want to devour."

"But I do want to eat you." He winked, and she blushed again.

Damn her traitorous cheeks. She needed to regain the upper hand. "You do realize, if you're not going to sign those papers, I am going to have you killed."

"Not going to do it yourself? I thought you were the type to see a job through."

"You're not a job."

"You're right, I'm not. I'm husband to a dangerous woman. Beautiful. Deadly. Did you know that your number of kills is unknown?"

"On purpose, but I can say it's more than a few."

His lips took on a rueful cast. "To think I ever believed you were so innocent."

"Not even close."

"I can't wait to see just how bad you can get." It

was then she realized she still held the knife in her hand. Yet she didn't use it. She'd had it pressed against his belly and couldn't shove it in. Frustration had her whirling and flinging it, sending it skimming past his head—which he didn't move by a single hair—to embed in the wall behind.

"Why do you want to die?" she asked.

"Who says I do?"

"Because you keep goading me."

"It's called flirting, baby."

"I don't like it."

"Get used to it."

"Or else what?"

He moved fast, so fast she didn't have a chance to escape his suddenly encircling arms. She didn't fight, she waited to see what he'd do.

He didn't do anything but flap his lips some more. It was getting frustrating.

"Why are you so afraid to be with me?"

"I'm not afraid," she said breathily.

He leaned in closer. "Your heart is racing. Your panties are wet. And we both know if we kiss again, we'll end up in bed."

His mouth hovered close enough that she almost gave in to his whispered temptation. She was saved by a knock.

"Go away!" she snapped.

"Are you and your husband awake?" Isa shouted back instead.

"What do you want?" Natasha pushed away from him to glare at the door, madness warring with relief at the interruption.

"Daddy wants to see you. And Dean."

"Why?"

Isabella didn't reply, and Natasha cast a glance at her husband. Bare-chested, in shorts and nothing else.

"You might want to sneak out the back," she noted.

"Afraid your uncle will shoot me?"

"I know he will if he thinks you'll cause trouble."

"And as a loving wife, that obviously bothers you."

"Keep annoying me, Neville, and see what happens."

"My name is Dean."

"Not according to your legal records." It was pure orneriness that had her calling him by his true name, Neville. It also helped with his already too sexy factor. "Get dressed and meet me in Uncle Vinny's office."

"What happened to me hiding?"

"It occurred to me that my uncle might be just what we need to solve our marriage dilemma."

"Is being my wife such a bad thing?"

Being his wife was a bunch of stuff, starting with confusing.

He sauntered off to the bathroom rather than wait for a reply.

The smug arrogance of a lion, the wily nature of a tiger. He was the most extreme of both breeds.

Stomping did nothing to alleviate her frustration,

but she did her best before knocking on her uncle's office door. When she'd previously explained her marriage dilemma, she'd made it sound as if it were a drunken escapade. It should have been easy to handle. Instead, she'd brought the problem to her uncle's home. She doubted he'd be impressed.

"Come in," Uncle Vinny shouted.

She opened the white door with its simple inlay and stepped into an office more cluttered and messy than expected. The walls were an array of mismatched bookcases and filing cabinets. Filled with binders that held sheaves of numbers. Vinny worked as some kind of hotshot accountant type. He made sure the family company—the legal and illegal parts—stayed afloat and kept out of trouble with the government. Her babushka claimed he was a wizard with numbers. Father didn't like Uncle Vinny but did begrudgingly admit the man knew his shit.

Uncle Vinny looked nothing as you'd expect. For beginners, he was blond, going on white, dressed in a light gray suit, no mustache, nothing Italian whatsoever about him. Was it any wonder her swarthy maternal grandfather had his DNA tested, not once, not twice, but five times?

Each time cost him a piece of expensive jewelry to a less than impressed Babushka. But the confusion was understandable given the rest of the family, including her mother, tended to be at least somewhat tanned and always dark-haired.

"You wanted to see me," Natasha said when he looked up from a ledger.

"Ah, niece, such a pleasure to see you. Where is your husband?" He said it lightly, but she could see the irritation tugging his brow. He didn't like unexpected changes to his routines.

"Dean will be along shortly. And you needn't pretend. I am aware you know each other. Why didn't you tell me?"

"It was old news. Besides, Isabella was the one to dump him."

Natasha found that hard to believe. "Sorry, I brought him here. I didn't know where else to go."

"A hotel comes to mind."

"I needed to keep him close by until he signed the divorce papers," she blurted.

"And, what? You couldn't find a pen?"

"More like he won't sign them."

"Won't?" Her uncle lifted both of his brows. "Didn't you say you were going to shoot him if he refused?"

It took effort to not bite her lower lip. "I was going to. But then we were attacked."

"By whom?" Her uncle immediately focused on the news.

She shrugged. "I don't know. They got away."

Vinny arched a brow. "Escaped you?"

"And me," was the unhelpful remark by her husband as he slipped into the room. "Bastards blew up my cabana!" he exclaimed, exploding his hands. "Cost me a bottle of good whiskey, too."

"The man is under attack, and you brought him to my house?" Vinny fixed her with a flat stare.

"I didn't know where else to go."

"Again, why couldn't you stay at a hotel?"

She batted her lashes as she said, "Because you have much better security." As her uncle glared, she continued, "And you love me because I remind you of my mother."

Vinny sighed. "I assume you caught the assailants."

"Not exactly," she said, hedging.

Uncle's wily gaze bounced between them. "Let me guess, you were too busy with your reconciliation."

Vinny totally misconstrued the events. "Never! I still intend to divorce him," she hastened to explain.

"Back to these attackers. Who are they? Who were they working for? Were they after him or you?"

She shrugged. "I don't know. Dumbass over here thought he caught one, but they got away."

"Shitty knots," Neville said with a shrug, looking not in the least discomfited by the fact that he was being grilled by her uncle.

Vinny leaned back in his chair and steepled his hands. "While all that is well and good, I still don't understand why he's here."

"I need him to sign the divorce papers."

"But you just said he wouldn't."

"He doesn't have a choice!" She scowled at her

husband, who smiled as he said, "Says you. You're the one who wants a divorce."

"Don't you?" Vinny inquired, gaze bobbing between them.

"Not really. I'd actually prefer if Natasha played the part of a real wife, then I wouldn't have to deal with the single ladies trying to put a ring on this." He held up his bare, left hand.

"Not that hard to buy one at the store." Vinny had a reply.

"A fake?" Neville put a hand to his chest. "Perish the thought."

"What happened to the ones at the ceremony?" she asked. Because he'd had a pair tucked into his pocket. He'd shown her the bands the night before.

"They suffered an unfortunate incident. It didn't feel right to replace them without my dear wife's input. Not to mention, I wanted it to match the engagement ring."

"I got rid of it." A lie. It was tucked inside a piece of fabric in a jewelry box at home.

"No matter, we can always go shopping for a new set."

"Is he serious?" Vinny asked, then eyed Neville. "You can't stay married to her. She's engaged to someone else."

"Technically, she can't be, as she and I had a prior and current commitment."

Vinny turned from him to Natasha. "Have you not explained what will happen if your father finds out?"

"You mean the fact that my papa will probably hunt him and have him mounted as a trophy?" She rocked on her heels. "If he's done his research as he claims, he knows."

"Do you want to die?" Vinny asked bluntly.

"People keep asking me that, and the answer is no. But I am a man of my word. I promised until death do us part."

"And death is going to happen, you idiot, if you keep stubbornly refusing."

"Does this mean you're ready to talk numbers?" Neville innocently inquired.

"What's he yammering about?" Vinny's gaze narrowed at the word *numbers*.

"He wants alimony."

"How much?" Vinny asked.

Her husband named an outrageous sum. She was ready to say no when Uncle Vinny said, "Done. Now, sign."

"I want the deal in writing," he insisted, which took an hour because they needed a lawyer to amend the contract. During that time, her husband went to eat. She followed, convinced he was up to something.

He made the most beautiful sandwich. Layers of meat, cheese, with hints of Dijon mustard in between.

By the time it was done, it required an unhinged jaw to take a bite.

She stuck to a healthy salad mostly out of spite—which her belly didn't appreciate.

Not much was said as they ate. Mostly because she was annoyed. Not that her uncle had agreed to pay, but more because, apparently, there was a price on Neville's supposed loyalty to his vows. She might not have liked it, but she respected him more when he refused.

After their meal, they returned to her uncle's office and the new divorce agreement. Neville made a show of reading it thoroughly, then signing it without looking at her once. Slid the documents back in the envelope and handed them to her.

Then, he left. Without a word. No goodbye or final lingering glance. Nothing.

As if she didn't matter.

And she hated that it bothered her. A lot.

It figured Uncle Vinny felt an urge to open his yap.

"What a shame your father has his sights set on that Simon cub. The tigon's got balls."

"He lacks common sense."

"In my day, we called it being dashing. A pity he and Isabella didn't work out. I could grow to like that husband of yours."

"Ex."

"Are you sure of that?"

She waved the envelope with the signed documents, but as her uncle kept smirking, she frowned and slid out the contract.

"That feline mongrel," she exclaimed. He'd signed the papers all right, signed them with a note.

The first one said, *Never*. Followed by, *Later, baby*.

Screw later, she was going to kill him now.

CHAPTER EIGHT

What a beautiful day. The sun was shining, warming Dean's bare chest as he relaxed atop the Pride condominium. He'd removed his shirt and wore only his khakis and some sunglasses. No shoes. No weapons.

He didn't need any, not when his wife was tough enough for the two of them on her own. And he expected her to arrive any second now...

"Neville Horatio Fitzpatrick!" She bellowed his name as she spilled out of the elevator onto the rooftop.

It drew more than one lazy gaze—and twitched more than one tail. Drew a snicker too as someone taunted, "Neville, wasn't that the name of Garfield's dumb nemesis?"

"That was Nermal," explained Jodi.

"Then who's Neville?" asked Stacey.

Rather than reply, Dean remained lying in the sun, enjoying the heated rays from behind his shades until someone blocked the light.

"You bloody idiot!"

He remained prone with his lids shuttered.

She whacked him with a rolled-up sheaf of papers. "Don't you ignore me."

He cracked an eye to see the storm. "Hey, baby. I didn't expect you so soon. Did you miss me?"

"Are you a moron?"

"Not according to the intelligence tests they made me take."

"You said you were going to sign." She waved the papers.

"I signed."

"Not your name!" she snapped.

"Yeah, well, as nice as the offer was, I couldn't accept it."

"You're the one who suggested it."

"No, you asked me for a price. I gave one that seemed reasonable. However, that didn't mean I had any interest then or now in divorce."

"Asshole!"

He pushed up his glasses and gave her a lazy grin. "Baby, really, is that any way to talk to your husband?"

Any twitching by the watching ladies, ceased. You could have heard a hair drop, it got so quiet.

Until someone shout-whispered, "Did he just say they're married?"

To her credit, Natasha—and her big brass balls—didn't budge at all when over half a dozen golden gazes veered her way, some of them kind of menacing. It was impressive that she'd even made it to the rooftop. How had she run the biatch welcome committee gauntlet? Hopefully, someone had video footage.

Natasha tossed back her dark hair as if defying them. "Don't get involved," was her warning. "This is between me and this mangy cur."

"I'll have you know my fur is quite luxurious. Did you know Arik's wife has transformed one of the first-floor condos into a salon? She gives the best scalp treatments." A remark that met with more than one murmur of agreement.

"Stop being deliberately obtuse. You agreed to the divorce. You got everything you wanted."

He sat up and replied, more tersely than warranted, "What I want is to be married. To you, I should add, in case that's not clear." It got easier to declare.

"But I'm engaged to someone else!" Her temper flared, and she stamped her foot, but it was her words that drew the "ooh" from the watchers, and one exclaimed, "Quick, someone order some popcorn from the kitchen!"

"Better call it off because bigamy is still a crime in this state."

"This is blackmail. I don't want to be married to you."

Dean stood and towered over her. "Too bad. You're mine."

"Oh," was the responding swoon from everyone but his wife.

Natasha wasn't swayed. "I belong to no one."

"I have a marriage certificate that says otherwise."

All the eyes swung her way, and Zena, one of the few lionesses not trying to get in his pants, muttered, "Twenty bucks says she hits him in the gut."

"Fifty says they have sex before the day is over."

Wagers were tossed back and forth, but he ignored them. He didn't dare remove his intent gaze from Natasha.

"I won't be your wife."

"You mean you won't be Simon's wife. You're already Mrs. Fitzpatrick." He poked her with a verbal stick. And still, the claws didn't come out. She had excellent control despite her temper.

"I am going to murder you," she growled.

"I wouldn't try that if I were you. My Aunt Kari over there will lose her shit if you hurt me. I'm her favorite nephew." He pointed without looking.

"Just say the word, and I'll shred her for you, darling nephew," was Aunt Kari's cooed reply.

The threat only narrowed Natasha's gaze. "She can try. You can all try. If I go down, my papa will ruin you all."

"Who is her dad?" someone asked.

Holding her gaze, because only an idiot would look

away from a tigress in a rage, Dean replied, "Sergeii Tigranov."

"Did he say...?" The sentence was never finished.

Despite the entertainment value of watching him spat with his unhappy bride, the name, renowned especially in their circles, caused the lionesses watching to scatter. Even here, far from his base, the Tigranov family was known—to be merciless.

"I see they have more common sense than you," Natasha remarked.

"More like they heard the dinner bell. It's Taco Tuesday at the restaurant."

"Tacos?" She glanced wistfully at the door going down. It was too damned cute.

"With queso cheese sauce and homemade tortilla chips."

"Stop tempting me, I will not be swayed by food." She pulled a fresh envelope from her back pocket and waved it at him. "Sign the damn papers."

"No."

"What part of *my father will kill you,* do you not grasp?"

"Still a no. And who says I can't get your father to agree?"

"Try it, and you will end up with concrete feet, feeding the fish at our family estate."

"Do you think me so incapable? I can handle your father."

"Don't you touch my papa!"

"I won't hurt him. But I will have him agreeing to this union."

"That will never happen because he's not the biggest problem. I promised my babushka when I thought she might be dying that I'd marry Simon."

That more than anything sobered him. "Has she recovered?"

"Yes."

"In order to assuage her disappointment, I'll make sure to bring flowers when I meet her."

"You will do no such thing. I won't have you shocking her into a heart attack."

"What makes you think she'll be unhappy that you're already hitched?"

"Isn't it obvious? I'll be married to you."

"And? What's wrong with me? As you've already noted, I'm wealthy." His parents had died in his teens but left him two large life insurance policies, among other things.

"You're not a tiger."

"I'm half tiger."

"My babushka is a purist. She'll never accept you."

"I didn't take you for a coward."

She eyeballed him, up and down, more appraising than anything else. A heavy sigh escaped her. "You won't stop until I agree, will you?"

"You need to be married, and I don't believe in divorce. So, why not make this work for both of us?"

"This will get ugly."

"You think Simon will cry?"

"Who cares about Simon. My papa won't be happy if Babushka gets upset. Hell, I don't want to upset her either if she's really dying."

"I'll deal with her. Women love me."

She snorted.

"Trust me."

Famous last words, right next to *"hold my catnip."*

Whump. Whump.

The steady beat signaled a helicopter overhead, not exactly uncommon in the city where many of the tallest buildings had pads. However, this one appeared to be swooping in on the Pride's condominium, which didn't have a landing spot. It should also be noted that regular helicopters usually sported a logo of some kind, indicating who they belonged to: nosy news networks, pleasure rides, a company that could afford a private chopper to fly its top cats around.

The whirlybird dipping ever closer appeared matte black and sleek. It also sported machine guns that dropped into place and began sparking as they fired.

No need to yell, Natasha was already moving, running for cover as bullets peppered the concrete roof deck.

Dean zigged and zagged after her, playing a game of dodge the slugs. In a moment, he'd ducked behind the tiki bar. A flimsy shield at best. The helicopter hovered overhead, and they heard the rub of gloves on nylon as people rappelled down.

He glanced at Natasha, who looked about as scared as a tiger confronting a den of rabbits. Meaning, she grinned and had a weapon in each hand.

"Ready?" she asked.

Before he could even think of replying, she stood and began firing, her revolver capable of piercing the body armor the men wore. But she was smart, rather than aim for kill shots, she maimed. Wrist holding a rifle. Kneecap, which was stupidly painful and effective at keeping someone down.

As for Dean, he didn't have a gun, just a stool and an old record in shot put. He swung the wooden seat up and over towards the helicopter, the furniture catching in the blades. Splinters rained down, and metal groaned. The chopper listed but quickly righted itself, and those machine guns began firing again.

At Dean.

He ran for the bullets instead of from them, keeping them trained on him, grunting as one managed to thud into the meaty part of his arm. He grabbed another stool in passing, and swung again, no sooner realizing it than he had a small metal side table.

Gronk. The squeal of metal proved loud, and the effect even bigger. The helicopter leaned as it lost control with its now-crooked blades. It listed, and as it went past the edge, the harnesses attached to the shooters dragged them along, out of reach.

Aunt Marni suddenly emerged on the rooftop, cracking a whip that wrapped around the leg of the chopper. She dug her feet in, but the moving heli dragged her along. The other lionesses that poured onto the deck grabbed her, and they tried to apply their combined weight to slow it. Only to suddenly tumble and land in a heap as one of the mercenaries shot at the whip, severing it. The chopper flew off, taking with it the breeze that ruffled Dean's striped locks.

He planted his hands on his hips and stared.

"Who were those brazen thugs?" asked his aunt.

"Who dares attack the Pride?" asked another.

A good question. What kind of idiot did that?

It was Luna who announced it first with a grim expression. "I think someone just declared war."

CHAPTER NINE

An hour later, pacing the lion's king's boardroom full of big, golden-haired folks, and one striped fellow, Natasha still couldn't believe the brazen attack.

"I want to know who sent them!" It was Arik, the Pride leader, who roared to cut through the din.

"We're working on it," one of the few dark-haired women replied. Melly something or other. "So far, we're coming up dry. The chopper had no markings, making it really hard to trace."

"You won't find anything. They were covert ops," was Neville's contribution.

"How do you figure that?" someone snapped.

"Because not only were they well equipped, but they were also smart enough to leave no traces," Natasha declared.

"No one asked you." An older woman, an aunt of Neville's, said with a glare.

"Why is she,"—a younger, blond lioness jerked her thumb at Natasha—"still here?"

"She's probably the reason those idiot humans attacked. She's a Tigranov, after all." Said by yet another aunt as if it were a dirty thing.

"Watch how you speak about my wife," Neville uttered in a low growl.

Arik slammed an open palm on the massive table. "Natasha Tigranov is here because we owe her an apology for not protecting her while enjoying Pride hospitality. She also deserves our thanks for helping out. Not to mention, being married to Dean makes her one of ours now." His glare around the room dared anyone to argue.

"But she doesn't want to be married to him."

"That's just a misunderstanding, Aunt Kari," Neville declared.

"That, or she obviously lacks taste," sniffed his Aunt Loretta, who'd sidled close before the meeting and whispered, "Always wanted a striped fur coat."

"If she doesn't want to be hitched, I can fix that problem," muttered Aunt Marni, drawing Neville's angry glare.

"For your information, Natasha and I have decided to give our marriage a proper chance. Which means, I'll need to borrow a jet."

"Going on a honeymoon?" Aunt Kari said with a sarcastic roll of her eyes.

"Honeymoon. Bachelorette. Meet the parents.

Natasha and I have some catching up to do, which will, at the same time, hopefully force whoever is attacking us to follow, giving us a chance to decipher the motive behind it."

"Do you really think it's wise to leave, given what's happened?" The only sane one in the room, Kira, asked. Must be her human genes that made her reasonable.

Neville shrugged. "If they are after me, then leaving here will remove the problem from the Pride."

"Attacking you is still attacking the Pride," Arik reminded.

"I'd rather it happen somewhere a little less likely to get someone hurt."

Luna snorted. "No one got hurt. They were shooting blanks."

Literally. At the time, they'd been too busy ducking to notice that the machine guns were armed with rubber bullets. Stingingly painful but not murderous by any means. She wondered if they regretted that choice, given she'd wounded them with the real thing.

"The bomb at his house wasn't a fake," Natasha noted.

"Who wants my nephew dead? I want a name!" Aunt Marni slammed her fist down.

"We're digging," Melly grumbled. "But we need a clue. I think Dean's idea of going off on his own is a good one. If he's the target, it will draw them out, and if he keeps moving, they'll have to act on the sly instead of having time to plan a proper ambush."

"Why attack at all if they're not even going to use real bullets?" asked Arik. "And how are we going to stop this from happening again? I won't have my people vulnerable to another attack."

"Working on it, boss," Melly muttered. "Implementing an airspace warning for any unidentified aircraft that comes too close."

"Include drones," Neville remarked.

"I want even kites shot down," Arik rumbled as he paced. "We need to send a message to whoever dared that this kind of incursion is unacceptable."

"Yes, sir." When the king spoke, everyone replied. Arik turned back to Neville. "When do you want to leave?"

"As soon as possible. Let's not give them time to regroup."

"I'll have the jet prepared at once. Luna, he'll need a security detail," Arik commanded, but Neville shook his head.

"I don't want them tagging along with us."

"I'm not sending you alone." The king sounded firm on that point.

"I won't be alone." Neville glanced at Natasha. "I'll have my very capable wife."

The compliment amidst his own people warmed, especially the many scowls thrown her way.

"How do we know she's not the reason we're

suddenly having problems?" Aunt Loretta asked. "After all, look who she's related to."

"Oh, if it were my papa behind it, there would have been no condo left standing. He's not one for half-measures or subtlety," Natasha announced.

"Tigranov would never do anything to imperil his daughter. This attack is some kind of message. And I want to know what it means."

The meeting might have continued except for the urgent buzzing that suddenly afflicted more than one cellphone.

Not being in the communication loop meant Natasha leaned over to read off the screen the human Kira held beside her.

There were cops at the condominium gates demanding entrance. Apparently, they'd received a tip about a drug lab in the basement.

Which led to some frantic relocation of the cages and other zoo-like equipment they kept down there for the occasional problem shifter. While the pride was busy convincing the cops that nothing weird was going on, Neville and Natasha, along with some hastily prepared luggage, were bundled into a sedan with blacked-out windows and on their way to a private airstrip.

She spent most of that trip on her phone. Sending texts, her fingers flying. His few attempts to talk were rebuffed with a look. She wasn't ready to speak to him yet.

She was still trying to come to grips with the fact that she'd agreed to his plan to remain married.

What was she thinking? Her father would never give his blessing. Babushka would probably die at the shame of Natasha marrying a half-breed. And the family would celebrate the tsarina's fall from grace.

Her idiot husband wasn't content to remain quiet. "Is it me, or was that the most pathetic attack ever?"

"I don't know that I'd call it pathetic. It certainly got our attention."

"But accomplished what? They obviously weren't out to harm us, or the bullets would have been real."

"Do you think it was the same group that planted the bomb at your place?"

"Maybe?" He shrugged. "Seems unlikely there are two factions out to kill us."

"Us? Don't you mean, you?"

"Both times happened when we were together," he pointed out, looking relaxed on his side of the car, wearing a loose, untucked button-up shirt, and comfortable khakis.

"Coincidence."

"Is it? I find it odd that we've now survived two attacks without any true injury. Brazen ones too, I might add. First, in my home. Then on Pride land."

"Someone trying to goad the Pride into acting hastily?" she suggested.

"My aunt thinks their goal was to antagonize your father."

"I'm just as deadly when annoyed," she grumbled.

"Adorable, too."

She shot him a dirty look.

"That's the look I love, baby." He winked.

"Keep acting so blasé, and you won't have to worry about meeting my papa."

"Why are you so afraid of that happening? Worried he'll give his blessing?"

That brought a wry chuckle. "More like I'll hate having to kill your aunts when they come after my papa for revenge."

His laughter proved genuine and rich. "I can see our family holiday dinners will be interesting."

"You don't say. Hope your stomach has an iron lining," she muttered because her aunt Rafaella could be liberal in her use of spices. Especially poisonous ones.

The trip to the airstrip occurred without incident. She remained on alert, and despite Neville's nonchalance, she didn't doubt for a moment that behind his insouciance, he would act at a millisecond's notice.

She still had no idea which of them was the target. It would be easy to assume her husband, and yet, what if she were wrong? Could the attacks be aimed at her?

The jet waited for them on the private airstrip, painted a golden color with the Pride Group logo painted in black on its tail.

She still couldn't believe she'd agreed to his insane idea of staying married, of going against her family's wishes. Before they went up the steps, she turned to him and decided to give him one last warning.

"Are you sure we should do this? It's not too late for you to sign the divorce papers."

"I might not have an easy time knowing what flavor of ice cream I want for dessert, I mean, should a person ever really choose between mint chocolate chip and caramel swirl? But in this, I am one hundred percent sure. Let's go meet the family."

She shook her head. "You'd better not blame me if you end up chopped into little pieces and fed to the hogs."

"Don't worry about me, baby."

Baby. Ugh. She had a love/hate relationship with the endearment. On the one hand, it was degrading to her as a woman. She was not a child. She was a killer, a businesswoman, strong and definitely not in need of a keeper. On the other hand, Neville knew all those things and still saw her as a woman and treated her like she was the sexiest thing he'd ever seen.

She kind of enjoyed that part.

What she didn't like was the way the sluts kept eyeballing him everywhere they went. First on the rooftop, then down in the lobby when they descended. Those same ladies, plus a few others, lounged and eyed them, some with blatant interest, while others lasered her with death glares.

When Neville wasn't looking, she made a rude

gesture and made it clear that he was her man. For the moment.

Despite his bravado, Papa would kill him. And if he didn't, Babushka surely would. Neville's days were numbered, which in a sense kind of relaxed her enough to realize she had nothing to lose.

Except maybe a chance for pleasure.

They boarded the craft, and her husband was the one to seal it shut. The pilot was already locked in the cockpit, making announcements. "Flight will be departing for Italy in the next ten minutes. Please buckle in."

She eyed Neville. "Italy? I thought we were meeting my family. My dad is in St. Petersburgh right now."

"But didn't you say your bachelorette was happening tomorrow night?"

"Yes, but I was going to cancel it since the wedding is off."

"You'd better not, and don't do anything to cancel the ceremony either. The first time we tied the knot, we did it quickly without anyone but Lawrence. No reason we can't have a grand ceremony for your family and friends."

She patted his cheek. "Your optimism about surviving that long is cute."

He grabbed her hand and held it against his skin. "I plan to live to a ripe old age with you, baby."

There went her heart, fluttering again. It pitter-pattered every time he smiled her way, held her hand and in general just existed. So annoying.

Of all the empty seats, he of course chose the one right beside her.

She waited for him to make his move. Instead, his hand still wrapped around hers, he put his head back and went to sleep.

He didn't snore or fall on her to drool while he slumbered. But he napped soundly.

She, on the other hand, was wide-awake. She kept running various scenarios through her head of how she could present her husband. All of them ended with her as a widow.

She glanced at him.

It seemed a shame to waste the little time he had left.

She straddled his lap, and he rumbled, "What are you doing?"

"Consummating our wedding night." She began unbuttoning his shirt, and when they refused to coop-erate, there was tearing involved.

"I liked that shirt," he observed.

"Then you should have taken it off before I had to."

His chest shook as he chuckled. "Impatient?"

"Horny." She was honest.

"You couldn't tell me this a few hours ago when we had a bed handy?" he growled, his hands on her waist.

"The seats recline."

"We're not exactly alone."

"The pilot is busy flying the plane. If he values his life, he better not interrupt."

"I'll kill him if he tries," he replied.

"Only after we land, if you don't mind."

Arrive alive. A mantra to live by.

She lifted her shirt, revealing a demi-cup bra, with nipples that hardened at his ardent gaze. She tossed the top to the side. Leaving her in a bra and jeggings that molded her figure and allowed her to sit astride him, feeling the hard bulge in his pants.

She rocked against it, and he hissed. "Going to rip those off, too?"

"Maybe," was her purred reply before she took his mouth in a torrid kiss. If she thought she could control what happened next, she was wrong. He immediately took command of their embrace, coaxing her lips to open and then engaging her tongue in a duel for dominance. A slick slide of flesh on flesh that only served to rouse the heat inside.

She ground herself against him as they kissed, and his hands firmly gripped her hips.

"Still so damned sexy," he growled.

"Even if I'm a liar?" she taunted, breathing the words hotly against his mouth.

"Would you believe it makes you even hotter?" He kissed her again, this time a slow, sensual tease of an embrace that saw her fingers digging into his shoulders. She squirmed atop him, grinding against the hard ridge of his erection, noticeable despite his pants.

Leaning away for a moment, she unhooked her bra and tossed it. She bared herself to him and basked in the heated ardor of his gaze.

She arched her back and presented her breasts. He needed no other invitation. With one arm anchored around her waist, he leaned forward and placed his mouth over her nipple.

"Yes." She hissed the word as the molten tug of his mouth made her pussy clench. She squirmed and gasped as he sucked, taking her nipple directly into his mouth. He swirled his tongue around it. Nipped it. Sucked it again.

She mewled. Whimpered. She bounced on his lap. Cried out when he swapped sides. She enjoyed every minute he spent playing with her breasts, teasing them in turn until she could take no more.

She shoved away. "My turn." He wasn't the only one who wanted to play.

She slid off his lap to her knees and grabbed the waistband of his pants. He lifted his hips as she tugged and pulled them down, leaving him clad in dark underpants that bulged with his erection.

She tucked her hands behind her back and leaned forward, using her teeth to grab the remaining material. She tugged and freed his shaft. It stood at attention, thick and tempting.

She licked it, and he hissed.

His body shook.

Oh, the power.

"Don't move," she warned as she grazed her teeth over the silken skin of his cock.

He trembled.

She sucked him, and he moaned.

When he would have grabbed her hair, she growled. "I'm in control."

He growled back. "I'm going to lose control if you don't stop."

Her laughter vibrated against the flesh of his shaft as she took him into her mouth. The salty drop pearling at the tip flavored her large swallow. How she loved the feel of him in her mouth. She worked her lips up and down the length of him, dragging them over sensitive skin, tasting every inch. He pulsed and shook as she sucked. His breathing turned harsh as she bobbed up and down.

She could have had him come in her mouth. But she wanted more than that. She needed him inside her. Needed the orgasm only his cock pounding against her g-spot could give. Quickly, she stripped her pants, then she straddled him once more and positioned herself over his cock. His hands were on her hips, but he didn't guide her. He let her choose the pace, and she chose slow, as in she lowered herself bit by bit onto his shaft. He stretched her nicely. She dug her fingers into his chest as he went deep. And deeper still until he was buried. Pulsing.

Oh, my.

Still in no hurry, she rotated her hips, grinding herself on him, feeling him butt against that sweet spot inside.

The hands on her hips helped her find a rhythm, a rocking and rolling, grinding thrust that coiled her pleasure higher and higher until it peaked.

And she might have screamed, but he caught the sound with his mouth, dragging her in for a kiss as his hips continue to pump, driving into her, drawing out her orgasm until she collapsed on him with a contented moan.

She eventually rolled onto the seat beside him—or tried to. Instead, she ended up on his lap, cradled in his arms. He pulled an airplane blanket over her.

"I should get dressed."

"Later."

Sound advice given they had sex twice more, the last time with her hands braced on a seat, and him plowing into her from behind. Slamming, his fingers digging into her hips as he pounded until he came, growling, "Mine."

And she allowed herself to enjoy the concept until they landed, and reality intruded.

CHAPTER TEN

Mile-high fantasy achieved. Now, if only his bride didn't look as if they were about to attend a funeral. Namely, his.

On the taxi ride to their hotel, they didn't say much. Natasha kept trying to hide her anxiety and yet gave herself away every time she looked at him, her teeth gnawing at her lower lip. She worried about him, indicating that she cared—more than she would admit. Slowly but surely, she softened. Hell, she'd melted for him on the plane.

It didn't matter that she'd seduced him because she remained convinced that he was going to die the moment she announced to her family they were a couple. Little did she know they'd been trying to kill him for months. At least, he assumed it was her family sending the thugs, given it started not long after he began looking into his duplicitous wife.

The first attack was made to look like a mugging. The thug jumping out of an alley wearing a ski mask and brandishing a knife. It was rather insulting as attempts went. He quickly disarmed him, but the attacks kept coming.

He tried going easy at first. Beating those that thought to ambush soundly. The one that stalked him, he'd had arrested on outstanding warrants. The waves of attack got bolder and more intense, including a poisoning of his pool water, which he had to admit was brilliant. Having a drone drop the chemicals was a stroke of genius. Problem was, he could smell it. He installed measures against future attempts and finally got serious about tracking down who was behind the attacks. He came up empty-handed. Whoever was hiring the humans did so under a complete cloak of secrecy. It was very impressive. It took deep pockets and a sharp sense to be so discreet. A mobster would have that kind of power.

But would Sergeii have put his daughter in danger? Sure, the rubber bullets wouldn't kill, but they'd sting, not to mention, accidents could happen. He found it interesting to note that the last attack had actually been the least dangerous. The explosion at his cabana could have seriously harmed her.

If it weren't Natasha's father, then who else would have the incentive to come after him? After all, attacking Dean was like poking at the Pride.

Arik might be easygoing in some things, but when

it came to the safety of his people and the care of his hair, he didn't screw around.

It would be interesting to see if the attacks stopped now that Natasha was involved. Or would it take meeting her father to end the game?

One way or another, it had to stop. It was one thing to threaten Dean. They crossed a line when they could have hurt Natasha.

They made it to the hotel without mishap, where he paid for their room and then went up to the second to last floor via an elevator. Rather than enter their room, he took Natasha past that door and into the stairwell.

"Why are we going back down?"

"Muddling the trail, of course."

They skipped down the many flights of stairs and out the emergency exit into an alley.

"Where are we going?" she asked, glancing around, keeping an eye on everything. At least now, she didn't have her mouth and eyes rounded in fake wonder.

"You and I will be staying somewhere off the beaten path. A place only I know about."

"Hold on, why would we leave if you think they'll attack the hotel? I thought we wanted to catch them," she stated, glancing at the tall and luxurious building they were leaving behind.

"We will catch them, but I think it should be on our terms and somewhere a little less likely to have someone with their camera out." He weaved them through some alleys, most of them sporting strong cooking scents that would mask theirs in case non-humans tried to follow.

They didn't need to hail a cab to get to their destination. It was only a fifteen-minute walk to a home, the façade made of old, mortared stone, jammed between other similar buildings, in an older part of the city. The keypad by the door, painted a glossy black and trimmed in bronze, beeped as Dean entered the code to unlock it. Click. He swung open the thick panel before he turned and swept her into his arms.

"What are you doing?" she exclaimed.

"Isn't it tradition to carry a new wife over a threshold?"

"Only of our home."

"But we don't have a home together yet. Are we going to stay at my place? Or yours? Although, my notes indicate you spend more time at your familial home than the condo you maintain in Milan."

"Live together?" she stated, sounding puzzled.

"It is what married people do."

Her nose wrinkled. "I never actually thought about it."

"Not even with Simon?" He did his best not to sneer. To think she'd thought to replace him with that milksop.

"We agreed ahead of time that we could continue

to live as we chose. With, of course, open invitation to visit each other. With notice."

"Sounds less like a marriage and more like a business arrangement."

"Marriage is business. It's a merger."

He shook his head. "You can't be serious. Marriage should be about two people wanting to spend time together. Becoming the best of friends. Partners. And lovers."

Natasha stared at him. "If you believe that, then why didn't you sign the papers? We're not any of those things."

"Aren't we?" He arched a brow at her. "I enjoy spending time with you. We're already lovers. And here we are, partnering up to solve a mystery."

"I—" She frowned before saying, a little grumpily, "We're not friends."

"Aren't we, though? I trust you not to shoot me in the back or while I sleep."

"Gonna say that's a pretty low bar if that's your criteria for friendship."

The remark brought laughter. "Have I told you how much I admire your sense of humor?"

"It's called sarcasm."

"And you're quite good at it."

"Idiot." Said with warmth. She pushed at his chest. "You can put me down now."

"If you insist." He set her down, nudged the door shut, all while keeping an arm around her waist.

She craned to peek at the barrel vault ceiling. "Cute place."

The walls were a mixture of stone at the front of the house, brick on the inside, with sections covered in hand-slathered plaster. Thick wood trim hid most of the modern electrical wiring that ran through the place. The floors, stone slab for this level, wood planks for the upper one, were covered in a thick rug, a woven pattern using lots of red and gold. The artwork on the walls proved just as vivid and contrasted with the dark-stained furniture: a couch with fluffy cushions, a few deep armchairs, a dining set with six straight-backed chairs.

He guided her into the living room area and said, "This house belongs to a friend of mine."

"Meaning someone does know we're here."

He shook his head. "My friend is currently in South America and will be for the next four weeks."

"And you just happen to know how to get in?"

"Are you really going to argue when it suits our purpose?"

"What kind of security does this place have?"

"The kind that lets us know if someone is coming. There are also some weapon caches in each room. I won't insult you by pointing them out." He'd already seen how her gaze was taking in everything around them.

"You do realize if they can't find us, then they'll just wait for the bachelorette tonight."

"Assuming it's you they want. Guess we'll find out when we split for our parties."

"You going to do something public to see if you're the one who's popular?"

He dragged her close. "I am going to be so blatantly out in the open they'd be stupid not to try."

"Without backup?"

"Are you saying I can't protect myself?"

"The last two times we were attacked, I saved your butt."

"Because it's cute, right?" He grabbed hers and squeezed.

"Passable." She tilted a hand left to right in a so-so gesture.

"Baby, I'm hurt."

"I'm sure your ego will recover." She pushed away from him and began exploring, the entire main floor, even peeked out the back door to check out the enclosed courtyard. "Who owns the places bordering our oasis?" She pointed up at the windows overlooking it.

"Humans. So no sunbathing in the muff." Meaning, skin only, no fur.

Curiosity satisfied, she headed up the stairs. She went through each room thoroughly, including closets, showing a keen eye as she sussed out the hiding spots for the various guns and knives. The four-foot sword with its razor-sharp edge hid in plain sight, nestled in a pair of brackets over the guest bed.

Natasha threw herself on the mattress with a sigh. "Nice place. I hope no one blows it up."

So did Dean. He clapped his hands together and rubbed them. "Are you hungry? Because I am craving some freshly made pasta."

"I could eat."

He stripped off his shirt and flexed a bit when he saw her looking.

She tucked an arm behind her head, and her eyes shut halfway. "What happened to getting some food?"

"I don't know about you, but I could use a shower before I touch anything." His pants hit the floor next, and her gaze dipped lower. "Care to join me?" He entered the bathroom, an area both modern and old at the same time with the toilet water tank bolted high above and dangling a string. Above it, another cannister for the electric water heater.

The shower sputtered before spitting out all the cold stuff. He held his hand in the spray until it turned warm. He lifted his face to the water and didn't immediately move when she joined him, her naked body pressed to his back.

Mine. Possessive, and yet he couldn't help it. How could she not see how perfect they were for each other?

He dragged her close for a kiss that lasted a while under the hot spray of the shower. There was much panting and slippery fun as they soaped each other. When he spun her to face away, she braced her hands on the tile wall and tilted her ass towards him. She moaned as he entered her slowly from behind.

He wanted to feel every inch of her tight pussy. Moaned as her scalding flesh pulsed around him. She wiggled her hips, seating him deeper. And then she goaded him.

"Going to just stand around all day or make me come?"

He'd make her come, all right. He'd make her climax so hard, so intently, she wouldn't be able to walk straight after.

In. Out. He began to pump, slipping in and out of her welcoming sex. He held her by the hips and thrust over and over again, feeling her tightening around him. Hearing it in the way her breath grew ragged.

When he felt himself getting close, he reached for her clit and rubbed. Circled his finger on that nub as he kept slamming into her. This time when she came, she could scream as loudly as she wanted.

He reveled in her pleasure and felt his own body tightening in reply. When she rolled into her second clenching orgasm, he joined her. Fucked her good and hard and growled, "Mine."

When they both stopped shuddering, he spun her into his arms and just held her.

Could have held her forever if her stomach hadn't growled, and she'd grumbled, "Married to a chef, and yet I'm starving."

The laughter proved vigorous. "So sorry, wife. Let

me fix that." He exited the shower, towel-dried, and headed downstairs.

She called after him. "Wait, I think you forgot something."

He glanced back at her. "I have everything I need in the kitchen."

"What about some pants?" She pointed.

He smiled. "I prefer to cook in the nude. Join me in the kitchen if you'd like to watch."

To his delight, she came down wearing nothing at all and, for the first time since he'd started cooking, he burned something. But it was worth it to have her eager and flushed on the counter.

Given he'd barely managed to put together food for one meal, and he'd ruined it, they ended up ordering in. It was after, with their bellies full, that her phone rang, and her smile slipped.

"What is it?" he asked, ready to leap over the table and reach through that phone to kill the person who'd taken away her happy face.

"Simon."

"I see." He said nothing but took the napkin from his lap and folded it before placing it on the table.

"I should take this."

She took the call outside the room on the balcony, and he resisted the temptation to go listen. When she returned, she appeared bemused.

"Everything okay?" he asked.

"I guess. I told Simon the engagement was off."

"How did he take it?" Because he knew how he'd react, and it would require a lawyer and bail money by the time he was done.

"Politely. He told me he understood what a difficult position I was in, and that he respected me for coming clean and wished us luck with our marriage."

"That's a good thing."

She grimaced. "I think he's lying."

"Is he? Maybe he wasn't keen on the whole getting hitched thing either, and you gave him the out he needed."

"I don't know." She looked skeptically at her phone.

"What's your gut say?"

"That he expected me to call it off. He didn't act surprised one bit. Didn't even argue."

"Would you like me to pay him a visit? Find out if he's got a secret."

The offer startled her. "No. Of course, not. He's not even close by."

"If you change your mind..."

She shook her head. "I am probably imagining things."

Still, her worry proved contagious, and no amount of sex—in the bed, on the kitchen counter or in the shower—made it go away. Although, each time he sank into her body, he lost himself.

He was ready to roar his affection to the world, to give her the hickey bite of all hickey bites.

She, however, remained convinced that after their sojourn in Italy, when they moved on to Russia to meet her family, that it would come to an end.

Which might be why he kissed her extra hard as the taxi arrived at the club where she'd be having her bachelorette.

"Don't have too much fun without me, baby," he breathed against her lips.

"Try and stay alive," was her reply as she got out.

He planned to live a long, long time. With his wife. He leaned forward and said to his taxi driver. "Take me to—"

The doors on either side of him opened, and bodies slid in just as the man in the front seat turned around and smiled.

"Surprise!"

CHAPTER ELEVEN

Entering the club, she had to admit being surprised that Neville didn't come in with her. In many respects, he acted the overprotective sort. Yet he didn't escort her inside and ensure the place was secure?

It didn't take the drawled, "If it isn't the striped cow who tricked our darling nephew," for her to realize why. He'd known his aunts were already here.

She would definitely kill him.

Natasha turned and smiled at his aunt, Marni. "You should stop acting so jealous about it. That kind of *love*,"—and yes, she finger-quoted—"is illegal in Italy."

Marni's lips pursed. "You're a sassy one."

"I think you mean I'm not a pushover."

"He could have done worse," Aunt Loretta

declared from her other side. "At least, she's a princess."

"Have you both forgotten who her father is?" huffed Aunt Kari.

"I haven't. I wonder if he's got a line on some good Italian wine for cheap," Marni mused aloud.

"Wine. Cigars. Illegal hunts. We are multi-branched and always open to new prospects."

"Such as?" The lionesses all eyed her. In many respects, they reminded Natasha of her own relatives. Shrewd, tough, and all about the family.

"Hair products. Right now, they're getting killed by tariffs. Greedy government," she declared. "Imagine if we could bypass those annoying rules."

The women smiled, showing way too many teeth, and Marni slung her arm around her shoulders. "I think we are going to get along just fine."

"Even if I'm a striped cow?"

"It's a compliment," Loretta declared. "Means you've got birthing hips."

Which was finally the thing to say to slam her mouth shut. She and Neville making a baby? She could hardly imagine, which might be why she drank way more than she should.

But she was among friends. Not only did she have the three aunts watching over her, they'd also brought a few of the renowned biatches, including Melly, Luna, and Stacey. Plus, Natasha's own friends showed, a handful with Ana, her dancer friend, whose blood was so diluted she'd only inherited the feline grace. Then there were her cousins Sasha, and Pietra. And two more friends from school, Bianka and Kloey.

Between them all, they put away a ridiculous amount of alcohol, traumatized the strippers given not one of them was truly bashful, and danced.

It should be noted that none of them ever actually got drunk. The watered-down versions sold in these types of places barely got them buzzed. Not that it mattered. No one attacked her.

They shut the club down, and then the aunts escorted her to their hideaway house, which was lit up and full of strangers.

Okay, not all strangers. She recognized Lawrence when he turned from the laptop some guy was working on at the kitchen table.

"What is going on?" she asked. "Where's Neville?" Because looking around, she didn't see his striped head.

"Who's Neville?" someone asked, only to shrivel under her glare.

"So, we might have misplaced your husband…" Lawrence started to say, coming towards her with his hands spread in apology.

She didn't need to say a word as Neville's aunts stepped forward. "Excuse me. Did I hear you say you lost my nephew?" Aunt Marni asked softly.

"Not exactly lost. It appears he might have been kidnapped."

"What?" Marni lifted Lawrence off his feet, which was impressive given he was a few inches taller and broader.

The other males in the room took note, but none came to his aid, probably because Loretta and Kari glared and kept them subdued.

Natasha was really starting to like these women.

She stepped closer to Lawrence, a knife in her hand. "You might want to explain, and quickly, how you lost my husband. Before someone gets hurt."

"When we heard what was happening, a bunch of us flew over to give him a bachelor party."

"Without warning him?" she asked.

"It was a surprise," Lawrence declared. "Jeoff over there wore some cologne to hide his scent, along with a wig and a hat." A fellow with short, brown hair waved. It took some squinting to recognize him as their driver from earlier.

"Good thing he was distracted, or it wouldn't have worked," Jeoff declared. "Should have seen his face when I turned around in the driver seat."

Lawrence took over again. "We told him we were kidnapping him and took him to a tavern."

"With strippers?" she guessed.

"We were trying to be authentic." Lawrence shrugged, and Marni sighed as she set him down.

"He didn't stay, did he?" his aunt predicted.

"No. The moment he saw the naked titties bouncing around, he was out of there like he'd seen a ghost."

"Breasts don't scare him," Natasha stated, only to blush as a few eyes turned on her. She angled her chin. "I'm sure he had another reason."

It was his Aunt Loretta who revealed the why. "His mother was an exotic dancer. It was how our brother, Manifred, met her."

"And now all strippers make him think of his mom," she concluded. "So, where did he go, and why did none of you follow?"

"We did. From there, we went to a billiards hall. Played a few rounds. He left a couple of games in to go have a piss."

"Alone?" she queried.

Lawrence shook his head. "I was with him. But I got distracted."

"Meaning someone shook her titties at him," mumbled the man who carried in a bowl of chips from the kitchen.

"And now, my husband is missing." She planted her hands on her hips. "This is unacceptable. We have to find him. Now."

"If it's any consolation, we don't think anyone took him."

"You said before you thought he was kidnapped." She sighed. "Why would he sneak away...?" She clamped her mouth shut. "He went to meet someone."

"Who?"

Given his sudden insistence on doing things traditionally, she had a sneaking suspicion.

She eyed her smartphone and, a moment later, dialed. It took three rings before someone answered.

"Tasha, my daughter. How was your bachelorette?"

"Fine, Papa. Do you have him?"

"Have who?" he asked a little too smoothly.

"Do you have my husband?"

"Don't be silly, Tasha. How can I have your husband when you aren't supposed to be married for another week? Or are we talking about your *other* husband? The one you neglected to tell me about."

Her stomach sank. "I was going to explain."

"You don't have to. I already know everything. Don't worry, I've talked to Simon and handled the misunderstanding between the two of you."

"You did what? I already spoke to him. He was fine with me calling off the wedding."

"But that was because he thought you were already married. A problem I am about to rectify."

"Papa." She injected a warning note in the word. "Don't you dare hurt my husband."

Rather than reply, her father, the tsar of the Russian Siberian Tiger Mob, hung up. She threw her phone hard enough that it shattered on the brick.

"Bad news?" was Lawrence's cautious query.

"My father has Neville."

And had more or less admitted he was going to murder him.

CHAPTER TWELVE

Waking up tied to a wall wasn't Dean's idea of a good time. Especially given it also involved a bucket of ice-cold water and a snarled, "Stop ignoring me, tiger!"

"Actually, that's tigon," he drawled, recovering enough to take a peek around. Old stone, low ceilings, naked lightbulbs. He appeared to be in a basement, and the man in front of him, wearing a thick pullover, with gray hair and an epic glare could only be one person. "You must be Natasha's father. I'd shake your hand, but I appear to be a little tied up at the moment." He was also feeling a little dumb. When he'd concocted his plan, probably while still lacking blood to his brain, he'd thought it brilliant. Contact Natasha's father and come clean about their marriage so he could get the man's blessing and finally put Natasha's fears to rest.

That was his plan as he left the bar without a word to his friends, not paying enough attention. Meaning, he got kidnapped for the second time that night. But, on the plus side, now instead of a phone call, he could talk to his father-in-law in person.

"I'd lose the arrogance, half-breed. You will pay and dearly for what you've done."

"That seems a little over the top, don't you think? I understand I'm not the son-in-law you expected, but—"

"There is no but. You married my daughter under false pretenses."

"Don't you mean she married *me* under false pretenses?" Danger, schmanger. He couldn't help but taunt.

"Either way, I didn't approve the match."

"With respect, sir, I don't think you get to decide who she marries."

Tigranov looked down his nose at Dean, which was rather impressive given his shorter stature. "I am her father."

"And a man who obviously respects his daughter. Why else teach her to defend herself so well? Why the fine education and positions of power within your empire? That kind of father doesn't tell his obviously capable child who she must be with for the rest of her life."

The older male's gaze narrowed. "She is a Tigranov, meaning the bloodline must be preserved."

"It also shouldn't be allowed to stagnate. Marrying cousins, even a few times removed, never ends well," he said, reminding Tigranov of the unfortunate murder-suicide in his family. Dean had done his research.

"You dare insult?" The angry man bristled, and hints of his tiger emerged. Not because he lost control but because he had a good grip on his beast. It took skill to have only bits of the body shift. In this case, Tigranov chose to menace with sharp teeth and claws, and a hint of whiskers.

"Can't handle the truth?" He arched a brow.

"Insolent, half-breed. I'll have you shot and mounted as a trophy."

"And then what? Marry your daughter off to the boring Simon?"

"Simon or someone else. I don't care who she marries, so long as it's not you." Brows beetled as Tigranov snarled.

Dean wasn't impressed. "Natasha needs someone strong by her side. And we both know that's not Simon. She'll railroad him and wonder why she's miserable. She needs a man. A real one to challenge and support her."

"What makes you think that's you?"

"Because she is mine." Probably a tad possessive to be declaring to her father.

"And has Natasha agreed to this?"

"Not exactly because she's convinced you're going to kill me."

"She would be right," Tigranov stated, tucking his hands behind his back. However, there was a problem with his statement. If the mobster wanted Dean dead, he'd already be sinking in a lake somewhere.

"Getting rid of me isn't in your best interest."

"Threatening me?" Tigranov's turn to pretend surprise.

"You're a smart man. You'd have to be with the empire you've built. You know what kind of friction my death would cause within the Pride. You also aren't sure how Natasha would react."

Her father turned pensive. "She didn't kill you for a reason." Meaning, Tigranov needed to hold off in case he made her angry.

"How about instead of working against each other, we join forces?"

"A deal?" Tigranov eyed him with a little less rancor. "What would you bring to the bargaining table? You aren't exactly a son in high standing in your Pride."

"But I am close to the king, with many friends."

"An alliance with Simon would have given me access to the Arctic."

"I have connections that might be able to help. You could also think of me as a liaison between your mob of tigers and the lions. Imagine what an alliance with the Pride could do for your family."

"We don't need mangy felines helping us with anything."

"No, you do just fine on your own. But think of the bargaining power you'd wield if it were known that the two groups were aligned."

"It is all well and good you'd negotiate, but how do I know the king will agree? What if he doesn't? Then what?"

"Would it help if I said I owned a controlling share in a maple syrup company?"

"Quebec-produced maple syrup?"

He snorted. "As if there is any other kind."

"A wedding gift to my daughter," Tigranov stated.

"That passes on to our children, and if none, then returns to the Pride."

A soft chuckle met his words. "Don't you trust us?"

"Nothing wrong with a little bit of security to ensure you don't kill me right after the papers are signed."

Tigranov kept eyeing him. "Natasha might one day run the family empire."

"All the more reason for her to have someone neutral watching her back."

That made the mobster snort. "How are you neutral? You work for the Pride."

"The moment I got on that jet with her, I resigned. As of this morning, I have someone looking at homes for Natasha and me. A place in Russia within driving distance of you, and somewhere in Italy. Maybe by the ocean."

"Making all kinds of plans as if you expect to live."

Dean leaned forward, his turn to smile. "I intend to live for a very long time."

"If I let you. How do I know you're good enough for my daughter?"

"Because I will eradicate anyone who tries to harm her." Stated coldly and firmly.

Before Tigranov could form a reply, the basement door slammed open, and a body came flying down, leaping the last few steps. Natasha hit the floor with her knees slightly bent and a gun in one hand. The knife, in the other, flew, the blade of it only narrowly missing Tigranov.

He gaped at his daughter. "You almost killed me!"

"Consider it a warning. The next one won't miss." A new dagger appeared, clenched in her hand.

The big, bad mobster held up his palms. "Tasha, my *zolotse*, calm yourself."

"Don't tell me to calm down," she snarled. "What are you doing with *my* husband?"

Dean took pleasure in hearing the possessive way she said it. He just wished he had popcorn as he had the impression that he was about to enjoy an epic fight.

"*Husband*? You don't say. Care to tell me something? Perhaps explain why you've been lying to me!" Tigranov puffed his chest.

"I was getting around to it."

"Too slowly," her father snapped.

"That didn't give you the right to steal Neville."

"Technically, he didn't steal me, baby," Dean interjected. "Your father just wanted to have a chat."

Her eyes, flashing with gold and green, glared at him. "He's got you tied to a wall."

"Just some friendly welcome-to-the-family hazing," Dean tried to say.

Her dad caught on. "Nothing nefarious. Just testing his mettle."

"His mettle is not your business."

That irritated her dad enough that he puffed out his chest. "You made it my business when you married him without permission and then hid the news from the family," Tigranov exclaimed.

"I was avenging my cousin's honor and did it by accident. When I found out, I immediately tried to rectify it."

"She did," Dean admitted. "She came and warned me to either agree to a divorce or she'd kill me."

"And yet, you live. Have you gone soft?" Tigranov asked, turning from Dean to Natasha.

"I thought he'd be more useful alive."

"Useful, ha. Do you know how easily we apprehended him?"

"And how many did you send?" she arched a brow as she neared. "Two thugs? Three?"

"Six, actually," Dean boasted. "But I didn't wipe

the ground with them because I wanted to meet your dad."

"Without me?" she snapped, stalking to stand in front of him. She waved a knife under his nose. "I told you he'd try to kill you."

"Good thing you love me enough to save me." He winked.

"No one ever said anything about love," she muttered.

"Yet, look at you, all worried."

"Not worried. I'm annoyed. At both of you." She whirled. "How dare you get involved?"

"I wouldn't have had to if you'd told me the truth," Tigranov retorted.

"Speaking of the truth, are you the one who sent those hit teams after us?"

"What?" Her father blinked. "Someone tried to kill you?"

"I don't know if they were trying to kill, given how bad the attempts were," she replied. "Did you send them?"

Her father stiffened. "First off, my elimination requests never fail. And two, I would never harm a hair on your head. I am insulted you would ever think I would."

"What about my head?" Dean queried. "Because the attacks started about a month after the wedding."

"Wait, what?" She whirled on him. "Do you mean the attack at your house wasn't the first attempt?"

"Didn't want to worry you."

She gnashed her teeth and glared at her dad. "Care to explain?

"Those attacks weren't ordered by me," her father declared. "I didn't even know about the half-breed until I saw the note."

"What note?" A placid expression on her face, Natasha said softly—and with deadly precision—"Have you been reading my private correspondence?"

"Well, that is, um..."

Wrong answer.

Dean jumped to the mob boss's defense. "A man in his position can't be too careful. His enemies might try and use you to get to him."

Tigranov shot him a grateful look.

"I am well aware of what his enemies are capable of. I'm the one who handles them." Natasha's jaw remained clenched.

"Can you blame me for being curious? You got mail from obvious Pride territory. I wondered why."

"And then proceeded to plot so you could meddle in my life."

"I just wanted to meet my new son-in-law," her father said, spreading his hand in a placating gesture.

"My husband is tied to a dungeon wall." She crossed her arms.

"Hardly a dungeon. Just playing. Ha. Ha." Her

father slashed through the ties binding his wrists to the wall. Dean stepped from it and gave her a smile.

"Look at you, being all worried for nothing. Your daddy and I are friends already."

"You're just saying that to get on his good side because he knows he's in trouble." Her gaze lasered on her father.

"Now, *zolotse*."

"Don't you even start with me. No more games. I want to hear you say you accept Neville as my husband."

"If it were just up to me, then...yes," her father said, however Dean heard the *but*.

"Who else do we need to convince?" he asked.

Natasha groaned. "My babushka."

CHAPTER THIRTEEN

Neville tried holding her hand on the last leg of the trip to her family home. It didn't ease the trepidation. She'd not expected him to survive her father. The tsar wasn't known for his benevolence.

She'd gone into that house expecting to find blood and maybe a body. Instead, two of the most annoying men in her life joined forces.

But that wouldn't help in the coming battle. Babushka was the one she'd made a promise to. She wouldn't care if Natasha was inconveniently married to someone else.

"It will be fine," he muttered, rubbing his thumb over the back of her hand.

"You don't know my babushka."

"I won over your dad."

"He's a pussy cat compared to her." She remained slouched, more nervous than she'd imagined being.

She loved her babushka. She was reasonably certain she loved Neville. What would happen if she had to choose?

Family, or her future? Hopefully, it wouldn't come to that.

Their car with its tinted windows had an entourage in front and behind, with Neville's aunts declaring that they wouldn't let him enter Russian territory without protection. Which, in turn, insulted her father into providing even more security.

They appeared more royal than the royals themselves. Her father might be a tsar in the tiger world, but in the human one, he was just a wealthy businessman.

She didn't pay much mind as they passed the wrought iron gates into the family estate. The big house that sprawled several stories and wings. More of a castle in many respects.

Upon entering, the servants were there to take their coats and offer them a warm, damp cloth to refresh their hands and faces. They weren't given the option to relax and change but taken directly to her babushka's room.

As in previous visits, her elderly relative lay abed under a thick pile of blankets, propped against fluffy pillows, her hair tucked into a cap that matched her voluminous robe.

"My dearest *vnuchka*." Her grandmother stretched fingers adorned with rings, and Natasha clasped them, bringing them to her lips for a kiss.

"You are looking well," she said.

"And you appear nervous." The old lady craned for a peek at Neville. "Could it be because you've brought a stranger to my bedroom? Why would you do that, I wonder?"

Shrewd Babushka knew exactly who he was. This was a ploy to get Natasha to admit what she'd done and apologize.

She'd do the former, but as for the latter... "I'd like you to meet Neville Fitzpatrick. Pride hunter, tigon, and my husband."

Babushka blinked. Waited. When no apology came forth, she coughed. "Oh, my heart. Shocking me in such a horrid manner. I feel weak." She put a hand to her forehead.

"If you're done?" Natasha arched a brow.

"Are you accusing me of being dramatic?"

"Yes, and of faking it. We both know you're not sick."

"A good thing I'm not. Showing up with a husband and not the one you were supposed to have." Babushka flung back the blankets and stepped out of bed. She also shed the gown and cap, revealing a cashmere sweater and slacks underneath. Her hair was perfectly curled. She slid her feet into her indoor shoes before heading for a chair by the hearth.

"I am not marrying Simon," Natasha stated stubbornly, following her grandmother.

"We'll see."

"I mean it, Babushka. Neville is my husband."

"For the moment. Leave us." Babushka waved her hand.

Neville turned to go, but her grandmother cleared her throat. "Not you. My granddaughter."

Natasha's eyes widened. "You want me to leave? But—"

A lasering gaze was all it took to have Natasha uttering a sigh. She leaned close to Neville and kissed him lightly on the mouth. "It was nice knowing you."

"I'll be fine, baby. You'll see."

She hoped he was right. Hard to tell what Babushka might do. Who would have thought she'd pretend that she was dying to manipulate her granddaughter?

Leaving the house, Natasha wandered down to the lake, arms wrapped around her body, ignoring the chill wind.

Gray skies roiled, and flecks of snow fell lightly. A storm rolled in, making her long for the balmier Italian climate she'd just left.

Then again, there was something to be said about lounging in front of a roaring fire. Naked. On a bearskin rug. With her husband.

She glanced back at the house. Would Babushka give her approval? Didn't really matter. Natasha loved Neville. With all her heart.

Movement in the woods caught her attention. A flash of red. How strange.

She wandered closer, strands of hair whipping across her face, the bite of an early winter in the wind's teeth.

The red item turned out to be a scarf, a silken thing wrapped around a branch. Had someone lost it? She reached for it, craning on tiptoe to pull the twig low enough to free the scarf.

She never saw the person wielding the club that knocked her down. She hit the ground on her hands and blinked at the leaf-strewn dirt. Whack. A second blow stunned her long enough that the attacker managed to tie her hands behind her back and place a burlap sack over her head.

They then tossed her over a shoulder and carted her away!

CHAPTER FOURTEEN

M*eanwhile...*
Dean eyed the old lady who sat straight-backed in her gilded chair. The tea service on the table was of the antique variety, lots of filigreed metal, gold highlights, and fine porcelain.

"Sit." The elder Mrs. Tigranov waved a bejeweled hand.

"Going to poison me?" Dean asked as she pushed a cup of tea towards him.

"Tried that. Not one attempt succeeded," she remarked as he took a sip.

He didn't spit it out, but he did put the cup down firmly. "You were the one behind the attacks." Stated, not asked.

"Yes." She calmly added honey to her cup.

"Let me guess, you tried to kill me so I wouldn't be married to your granddaughter."

She snorted. "If I wanted you dead, you'd be dead. Think of it as more of a test. After all, you didn't think just anyone would be allowed to marry my grand-daughter, did you?"

"You were going to let her marry Simon."

"Was I?" the matriarch asked with a smile before taking a dainty sip.

"Are you implying you weren't going to let her marry Simon?"

"No need for me to act when I knew you would."

He leaned back with a cookie in hand. "How did you know?"

"I knew about the marriage the night it happened, or did you think me unaware of her actions? I know everything that happens in this family."

"If you knew we got married, then why not say something?"

"Because I was curious to see what would happen. It was intriguing to see how interested you were in her actions. Or did you think your inquiries went unnoticed?"

"Did it never occur that maybe I sought revenge? After all, she did catfish me."

"She lied about some things, yes, but it's the other things she did that I didn't understand. She did not have to share your bed or plan a wedding to accomplish her revenge. She obviously liked you. More than any other man she'd set her sights on."

"She liked Simon enough to say yes."

Again, the old lady snorted. "I manipulated her into that. Mostly because, despite her also watching you, she wouldn't act. Neither of you was doing anything. I'm an old lady, I hastened the show along."

"You blackmailed her on a fake deathbed to get her to agree to marry Simon, knowing I'd see it and swoop in."

"It worked better than expected. You should have seen the tantrum she threw when your note arrived, informing her of the marriage. Natasha never loses control," the matriarch confided. "Any man who can make her feel so strongly obviously means something."

"She's my mate." It felt good to say it out loud finally.

"Perhaps. But I had to be sure you were worthy, hence the little tests, which you passed quite handily, I might add."

The old lady seemed pleased with her actions. "The bomb at my house a few days ago could have killed her," he growled.

"Bomb?" She frowned. "I never authorized any bombs. The last attack was the one on the rooftop with the blank missiles. Once I realized she was ready to defend you, I knew it was only a matter of time before you both came to me for your blessing."

"Hold on, if you didn't authorize the bomber at the house, and your son didn't either, then—?"

Aunt Marni barged in, hair askew, blouse buttoned crookedly. "I think someone took Natasha!"

"What?" He shoved out of his chair. "Explain."

Auntie held out an envelope. "This was found on the front step. Addressed to her dad."

"You dared open Tigranov correspondence?" The matriarch rose from her chair with a regal tilt of her head.

But Dean didn't care if she was insulted. He took the note his aunt pulled from the envelope and trembled as he read it.

Tigranov.

I have your daughter. If willing to negotiate for her, then kill her tigon husband as a gesture of good faith.

"Who would dare?" he roared as he let the sheet flutter.

It was Babushka who had a quiet reply. "I think I know who took her."

CHAPTER FIFTEEN

Natasha squinted as the sack came off her head. She blinked as she focused on the figure that stood in front of her. "Simon?" But not the gentleman she'd come to know.

Gone was the designer suit and vapid expression. His boyish, curly, white-blond hair was slicked back. He wore combat pants, a tight turtleneck, and steel-toed, matte-black boots. To finish his ensemble, a holster with both a knife and a gun.

She went to move only to realize that she was bound to a chair. She rattled it on its four legs and growled. "Let me go at once."

"No." The firm reply was at odds with the Simon she recalled.

"Exactly what do you think you're doing?"

"Getting the leverage I need to get what's owed. You were supposed to marry me, giving me access to your father's supply network. But, instead, you humiliated me by jilting me for a half-breed," Simon seethed.

"Kidnapping me isn't going to change that."

"No, but not killing you in exchange for what I'm owed is a fair deal."

"You won't get away with it."

"I already have. No one knows where you are. And they won't be able to track you." He swung open the door and showed her the swirling snow. "I have enough supplies for us to stay here for weeks. I figure it won't take more than a finger or two, maybe a few recordings of your screams before your family concedes."

"You really shouldn't have done that." She shook her head as the snow swirled inside the cabin.

"Your family doesn't scare me."

"It's not my family you need to worry about. It's my husband," was her reply just as a streak of orange and black fur came bounding out of the snowstorm.

Simon had a moment to turn before the tigon pounced on him. In a moment, a very fluffy feline wrestled with a striped white tiger and rolled out of sight.

Meanwhile, she was stuck. She rocked the chair, back and forth until it hit the floor and jolted. Not enough to fully break, but it did loosen the ropes. She managed to scrape her hands free and push from the chair just as the two cats tumbled into the cottage, their tussling bodies slamming into the table and sending it with its supplies toppling into the fireplace.

She flattened against a wall as the men continued to grapple, their large cats snarling and snapping while smoke filled the air.

Wait, smoke? A glance over at the fireplace showed it smoldering as the things that had fallen into the hearth caught fire. The most concerning was the smashed bottle of vodka that acted as fuel and sent the flames zipping out of the fireproof hearth. The dry plank floor began to smolder as she scrambled out of the path of the slamming feline bodies. She flattened against a wall and patted herself down, looking for a knife, a weapon, anything.

Simon had frisked her well, removing all her toys.

"Dammit." She'd gone away from the door instead of towards it and found herself trapped behind a growing wall of flame.

Seeing her dilemma, Neville suddenly released Simon and attacked the door.

She didn't understand why until it toppled, and he dragged it to the blaze, creating a bridge through the fire.

She ran across, the heat nipping at her skin and clothes, and had almost made it across when Simon slammed into Neville, which in turn knocked into her, driving her back into the inferno.

Heat licked and singed. She dove forward but could still smell the burning and feel the scorching as the fabric on her body burned. She dove out the open doorway into the blizzard. She hit the ground and rolled, hearing the sizzle of cold snow on burning fabric. As she lay on her back, face to the sky, the chill of the snowflakes refreshed her blistering skin. She lay there for a moment, just breathing, only to startle at a crash.

She sat upright and caught the cabin folding in on itself as the flames eroded its structure. "Neville!" No one emerged from the flames.

Oh. No.

"Neville." This time, she whispered his name, her throat thick with tears.

"I really wish you wouldn't call me that."

CHAPTER SIXTEEN

H is statement was met with a hollered, "You're alive."

Scrambling to her feet, Natasha ran for him, slamming into his bruised frame. Not that he complained. He gladly clasped her to him. He'd been so worried.

It was why he'd raced ahead the moment Mrs. Tigranov told him that they could track Natasha.

"You chipped the girl?" his auntie asked.

"Don't you love your family enough to always know where they are?" Natasha's grandmother retorted.

They started talking rescue party and guns. He'd taken one look at the beeping dot on the map, memorized the terrain, then stripped.

His mate was in danger. He couldn't sit and wait.

"Are you okay?" Natasha leaned back to check him over.

He offered her a crooked smile. "I'm not even close to using up my nine lives, baby."

"Where's Simon?" She craned to look past him.

"One minute, we were fighting. The next, he ran back inside the cottage."

"He killed himself?" She glanced at the inferno.

"Probably because he knew he was screwed." With the adrenaline beginning to wear off, he started to notice the cold. The blustery wind and snowflakes chilled his flesh. He could only imagine how his wife felt, her clothing damp and scorched almost through in spots.

He stepped back from her. "Let's put on our fur and get back to your house."

"I can't." She shook her head.

"Why not?"

"About the whole shifting thing... So, you might want to rethink the annulment because I might have neglected to inform you that I can't actually turn into a tiger."

"What do you mean, you can't shift?" He blinked at her and thought of all the times she'd... Huh. "I've never seen you change.

"Because I can't," she grumbled. "Not for lack of trying. My brother and sister can, and while the doctors say I've got all the right genes, something inside me just won't let the switch happen." Her shoulders rolled. "And trust me, my family tried everything to get it to happen."

"But you smell like a tiger." Her scent was unique, though.

"Yup. And the doctors seem to think my kids will be fine. I know I should have told you before." She shrugged. "I honestly thought my family would kill you, but now that they haven't, you should know before you make any promises."

He snorted. "Do you really think I care if you can sprout fur or not? I didn't fall in love with an animal. I fell in love with you." He dragged her close. "And I intend to be married to you until death do us part, baby."

"You say that now, and yet...what if down the road, on a full moon, you get pissed I can't follow you on a hunt?"

"Why wouldn't you be able to follow?" His brow crinkled. "Are you planning to gain a lot of weight and stop moving?"

"No."

"Then who cares if you're doing it on two feet or four. I love you, Natasha Marika Fitzpatrick."

"Tigranov hyphen Fitzpatrick." She rolled her shoulders. "I should probably keep it given I am the heir."

"So long as I can call you mine."

He kissed her and would have kept on kissing her if the rumble of all-terrain vehicles didn't disturb the snap, crackle, and popping of the fire.

In short order, she was driving a machine, while the original pilot sat bitch on the back. Her husband changed back into his fur, and they were off.

At the door to the house, too many family members awaited, all of them wanting to hear what had happened. Natasha wasn't in the mood.

"I'm cold and dirty. And going to my room, with my husband." Her challenging gaze dared anyone to argue.

When Daddy Tigranov glowered at Dean, he shrugged. He wasn't about to pick a fight with his wife.

The fire in the bedroom proved more than welcome. But even better was the tub someone had dragged out to sit in front of it and filled with steaming water.

He sank into that tub, leaned his head back, closed his eyes, and exhaled. "This is paradise."

Splash. His wife joined him, sloshing water over the sides before she grabbed him roughly by the cheeks. "Care to rephrase?"

He let himself gaze upon her, her teasing smile, the way her hair tumbled over her bare shoulders. "This bath is paradise, but you...with me? That's heaven."

He dragged her close for a kiss that spilled even more water onto the floor, not that they cared. Sex wasn't the easiest of things to do in a narrow tub, but they managed. He ended up on his knees, with her bent over in front of him, gripping the edge of the tub while he slid into her from behind. His arm curled around her waist, kept her body curved into his. He leaned in and bit the lobe of her ear as he thrust into her, spilling his seed only when she climaxed with his name on her lips.

"Neville!"

He would take his real name any day over the barked, "Get up," that came the next morning. Grandma woke him with a yell and a whack from her cane.

"Ow!" He glared.

"Get up. Out. Let's go."

"Go where?" He rolled from bed and avoided the Tigranov matriarch as she wielded her weapon."

"Babushka! Stop it." Natasha scowled as she clutched the sheet to her bare chest.

"No, you will stop it. Until the wedding. Ladies don't fornicate out of wedlock."

"But we're already married," Natasha huffed.

"Of a sort. I am aware of the pagan church you used. You will do it again. Properly and until you do, no more coitus. Get." The last came with a jab in his direction that he dodged.

There was no changing Grandma's mind, which Natasha grumbled about. However, having waited this long, Dean had no problem waiting a bit longer.

Her family had accepted him. The threat was gone. And he was about to marry the woman he loved in front of friends and family.

Since he had no living parents, his aunts gave him away with his aunt Marni leaning close to kiss him on the cheek and whispering, "Be happy, favorite nephew."

He planned to because a tigon wedded for life.

EPILOGUE

The wedding turned out awesome. Lions on one side, tigers on the other. Given the amount of partying that went on at the reception, it was expected that they'd see more than a few hybrids in nine months or less.

The only tense moment came when the priest asked, "Is there anyone that can show just cause as to why this couple cannot lawfully be joined together in matrimony? Speak now or forever hold your peace."

When it appeared as if cousin Isabella might open her mouth, the aunts, who'd chosen to sit behind her instead of with the lions, leaned forward, and Marni whispered something. Isa closed her mouth.

And they were wed, for a second time.

After a splendid wedding night where he took her in the limo, then the honeymoon suite bed, shower, and against the penthouse windows, they boarded a plane.

According to their social media posts, they were enjoying a romantic dinner on a beach in the south of France.

In reality, they were hunkered in tall grass somewhere in the wilds of Lithuania, waiting for some contraband cargo.

Natasha glanced at him. He wore his stripes, and in honor of their mission, she'd painted lines on her skin, too. Her eyes glinted with excitement. She smiled. "Ready?"

Always. He headbutted her as he rose. They were already moving as the wheels of the small propeller plane hit the pavement.

"Try and keep up."

"Grawr!" was his reply as he loped by her side. As if he'd ever lose her.

He'd found his mate, and she was everything he'd ever wanted. Friend. Partner. Lover.

MEANWHILE, *after the reception...*

The pinprick in Lawrence's arm was like the smallest of stings. There and gone, not even worth his attention.

But perhaps Lawrence should have minded it because his senses clouded, his vision filmed over, and when next he regained consciousness, it was to find himself in a strange cabin in bed with a woman.

A human and—judging by the scent on her and the marks on her neck—his mate.

Lawrence's story is coming next in When a Liger Mates.

LAWRENCE'S STORY IS COMING SOON IN WHEN A LIGER MATES.

Previous books in A Lion's Pride, a USA Today Bestselling series:

Be sure to visit www.EveLanglais for more books with furry heroes, or sign up for the Eve Langlais newsletter for notification about new stories or specials.